Death by Drop Spindle

by Tian Connaughton

A Hazel Whitmore Mystery

Table of Contents

Copyright

Connaughton, Tian.
Death by Drop Spindle
ISBN: 979-8-9876176-5-6 (ebook)
ISBN: 979-8-9876176-6-3 (paperback)
To learn more about Tian Connaughton, visit www.tianconnaughton.com.

Dedication

Dedicated to my husband, Daniel, and son, Aidan.

Books by Tian Connaughton

- The Magic Knitting Pattern Book (a novel)

- Cardigans For Every Body: because every body is worthy

- Unlock Your Inner Designer: How to start designing

- Pattern Launch Plan: Sell more patterns consistently without being sleazy

tianconnaughton.com/books

Prologue: Wednesday Evening

"**I** can't just ignore this. I won't!" the older woman declared, her voice cutting through the storm outside. Her arms were crossed tightly over her chest, her feet planted firmly on the creaky, weathered floorboards. The wind howled outside and rain lashed furiously against the window. The air charged with tension.

"You don't mean this." The younger woman's voice wavered, but not with sorrow. No, there was something else beneath it, something sharper.

The older woman forced herself to hold her ground. "I do."

"But you're my *mother*," the younger woman hissed. Her expression shifted, fury cooling to something measured, something dangerous. Not pleading. Calculating.

"So, this is it." Her voice softened, almost contemplative. "When I needed you, when she needed you, you did nothing." Her face twisted with betrayal. Though barely above a whisper, her words struck with the force of a slap.

A chill crawled up the older woman's spine, though she refused to shiver. She had prepared for anger. But this quiet resolve? This was something else.

"How could you do this?" she asked. Pent-up anger and heartbreak clung to every syllable, raw and unrelenting. What had she actually expected from her mother? Nothing! And once again, that's exactly what she'd gotten.

The two women glared at each other, eyes locked in a fierce standoff, each unwilling to surrender. The lines were drawn and neither were willing to give in an inch.

"I've never asked you for anything, except this. It's the very least you could do." The young woman pressed, but her voice faltered, and her bravado cracked under the weight of her emotions, the last words breaking apart like glass. She felt the prick of tears behind her eyes. She looked down and blinked them away. Her fists clenched and unclenched as she fought to steady her breath. She would never let this woman, her mother, know how much she has truly hurt her.

Mothers were supposed to protect their child and do anything to make them happy. This conversation wasn't just proof to the contrary; it was a searing reminder to reinforce what she'd always known—blood wasn't thicker than water, the younger woman thought, hot angry tears threatening to spill but she forced them back. She wouldn't give the older woman the pleasure of seeing her cry.

The older woman's face hardened, lines of anger and grief etched deep into her expression. She turned abruptly away from the younger woman, her entire frame trembling with a mixture of frustration and sadness. Her gaze shifted to the rain-streaked window as if searching for an escape into the dark night. The wind screamed and the rain pounded, echoes of their unspoken words.

It was late. She was tired. It had been a long day. She had to end this conversation. Exhaustion seeped through her like the dim light creeping around them. She shouldn't have let it get this far. She should have put a stop to it the second she found out. But she was trying to be a good mother. But that hadn't worked out. It had only made the situation worse.

Children often disappoint. People think a mother's love is unconditional. But there were limits.

"When Robynn needed you, you did nothing. You could have made a world of difference but instead you turned your back on her and me, just like you are right now. And in this moment, you have a chance to redeem yourself; to make amends. You have the opportunity to show me that it was all a mistake and, if given a second chance, you would take it all back. But this is the path you choose?" The accusation sliced through the room, sharp and deliberate, each word cutting with precision. She wanted to hurt the older woman, to pierce that cold and impenetrable armor. She wanted her mother to feel every second of the pain she'd caused.

The young woman tilted her head, considering. Then, she turned, shoulders squared, her steps deliberate as she moved towards the door.

The older woman exhaled, pressing her fingers against her temples. It was done. She had done the right thing. Hadn't she? She had thought it would feel satisfying, standing her ground. Instead, the silence gnawed at her.

The younger woman paused at the door, fingers tightening around the handle. She turned, her gaze lingering on the rigid line of the older woman's back, on the way she stood, straight and unmoving, staring into the night as if she had already turned her daughter into a memory. The realization struck like steel. There would be no last-minute redemption. No flicker of guilt. Just silence.

Her grip tightened. Her voice, when it came, was quiet but precise. "I'm sorry for you."

She didn't wait for a response. She opened the door and stepped into the fury of the storm.

The door clicked shut, not slammed, not rushed. A sound too careful. Too precise.

The storm outside raged on, but inside, there was a chilling silence.

The older woman didn't turn from the window. She stood frozen, watching cold raindrops race down the glass, merging and breaking apart like their relationship.

A flicker of instinct – drive carefully, the roads are slick – tried to claw its way up her throat. But she swallowed them down. What was the point? Concern was a performance she had no right to give. She couldn't play the role the younger woman wanted. The doting mother. It was too late for that.

They had gone through too much to go back.

The younger woman had made her choice. So had she.

Now, they would both have to deal with the consequences.

Chapter 1: Thursday Late-Morning

"**O**h, you're crocheting. My grandmother used to crochet. Isn't that a craft for old ladies? I didn't think anybody still did it."

The woman with limp, oily blond hair barely slowed down, her words trailing behind her like the clatter of her heels against the polished airport floor. Before Hazel Whitmore could muster a reply, the woman's thin, age-spotted hand darted out, patting Hazel's project with the kind of misplaced enthusiasm one might reserve for greeting a pet. Then, just as abruptly, she disappeared into the crowd.

Hazel blinked, the rhythm of her knitting needles faltered for only a heartbeat before she resumed the smooth glide of her stitches. The plain vanilla sock she was working on grew stripe by stripe under her practiced fingers. She was used to these moments by now, the unsolicited comments, the judgments, and condescension wrapped in feigned interest. People loved to make assumptions about her and her craft, to reduce her and her work as a quaint relic of a bygone era, as if she was some kind of curiosity on display.

Her outfit echoed her personality, an intentional blend of artistry and comfort. She wore a lightweight crochet pullover made from multicolor granny squares, each square a remnant from her past sock projects. Paired with fitted jeans that hugged her generous curves, brown knee-high boots, and a trench coat, Hazel's ensemble exuded both confidence and ease.

Her dark, natural hair, streaked with silver near the temples, was braided into two thick plaits that trailed down her back, a style she'd adopted years ago for its simplicity and sense of order. The overall effect was striking, an effortless balance of color, texture, and timelessness.

Standing just inside the sliding glass doors of St. Louis International Airport, Hazel blended into the crowd of travelers waiting for their rides. At barely five feet tall, she was easy to overlook. Clusters of people gathered near the doors out of the chill, scanning the curb for familiar cars, but Hazel stood slightly apart, hands moving steadily as she knitted. For those who cared to notice, there was a quiet gravity to her demeanor, a steady presence that belied her size. Her dark brown eyes, sharp and observant, took in bustling scene around her with a measured gaze, pausing now and then to glance at the flow of traffic outside.

The air around her thrummed with a low hum of overlapping conversations and wheels clattering over tiles. Above the dull noise, the relentless, almost sterile voice of the PA system cut through, announcing flights and issuing constant reminders: *"Please do not leave your bags unattended. Report any suspicious behavior to airport staff."* The announcements played on repeat, merging with the ambient noise into a soundtrack of urgency and motion.

Each time the doors slid open, a crisp autumn chill crept in, brushing against Hazel's cheeks like a cold hand nudging her forward, urging her to move. She let out a slow breath and paused her knitting, slipping the project into one hand as she clutched the handle of her oversized suitcase with the other, holding it a little too tightly. This was the biggest trip of her career, a pinnacle moment. At thirty-seven, she had finally become a rising star in the fiber industry after more than a decade of diligent work.

Her journey hadn't been easy. Hazel spent years working long hours juggling odd jobs to make ends meet while chasing her passion. For years, she'd designed crochet and knit patterns, first self-publishing them online before landing features in magazines and books. She had collaborated with yarn companies, crafting patterns to show crocheters and knitters what they could create with yarn, guiding them on a journey from curiosity to finished pieces. All of that effort, those years of sketching new ideas, frogging row after row to get the design right, and the late nights had led to this profound milestone: a published book and her first major event as a headliner.

Her fingers tightened around the soft yarn of her sock project as a loud burst of laughter rang out from across the terminal. Hazel glanced up and spotted the source: a group of people decked out in handmade sweaters, scarfs, shawls, and hats in a riot of colors and texture. They stood in a circle, excitedly showing off projects and admiring each other's work. One woman reached out to stroke the shawl on a friend's shoulder, her face lit with delight.

Hazel's chest tightened. She didn't recognize the people, but knew they had to be here for the retreat. She could spot a crocheter or knitter from fifty paces.

The group began moving, heading in Hazel's direction. Her heart pounded furiously, a sudden thrum of panic spreading through her chest. She turned away, her movements deliberate but not too obvious, angling herself toward the wall. She shrank into herself, instinctively making her already small frame smaller. She wasn't ready, not for this.

She focused on her breathing, shallow and rapid, trying to make herself invisible as the group passed. They didn't notice her. Relief washed over her, leaving her weak.

Hazel exhaled a long, shaky breath, still clinging to her sock project for support. She wasn't ready to talk about her book, about crochet and knitting, about anything. Not yet. She had planned to ease into the weekend, to slip into her role quietly once she arrived at the shop. Here, in this crowded terminal, she felt exposed, like a skittish animal out of its den.

Her eyes darted around the bustling terminal, seeking an anchor in the chaos. Her pulse still hammered in her ears, and she caught herself wondering, again, if she could really do this.

She had the talent. She knew that much. Years of hard work and quiet determination had brought her to this moment. But all the other stuff, the attention, the small talk, the endless smiles, was a different story.

Hazel pulled her knitting project close, as though the soft familiar yarn could steady her. She closed her eyes for a moment, drawing in a deep breath that filled her lungs and steadied her racing pulse. No matter the nerves fluttering in her chest, she knew one thing: there was no turning back.

Her phone buzzed. The third time, bringing her back to the moment.

Hazel glanced down at the screen, eyes scanning the message: *Your car is here. Black sedan. Driver's name is Marcus.*

She returned to her knitting, her fingers automatically finishing the row she'd been working on. The familiar rhythm of the stitches calmed her, grounding her as she steadied her nerve. After a beat, she slipped the sock into its designated project bag, her fingers lingering on the soft merino and nylon blend yarn for a moment, as if savoring the comfort it provided. With a sigh, she tucked the bag away in her purse.

"Showtime, Whitley," she muttered under her breath, her voice barely audible in the airport din.

Whitley. Her alter ego, her armor for events like this weekend. This was her ritual, a way to calm the nerves before stepping into another event, another retreat, another project. It was a quiet affirmation that she could face whatever was next. She was Hazel Whitmore, the practical crochet and knit designer, author, and teacher, but when it came to moments like this, Whitley was the inner strength that she put on like armor.

The Whitley persona was bold enough to say what she, Hazel, could only think. It was Whitley's confidence and steadying force she borrowed when doubts crept in, a reminder that even when her hands trembled, Whitley kept her secure and strong.

Unlooping a well-loved, woolen scarf from the strap of her handbag, Hazel wrapped it snugly around her neck as the chilly autumn air bit at her warm brown skin. This scarf had been the first pattern she'd ever designed, her initial foray into the industry. It stood out as the most valuable thing she'd ever made. It was a piece she cherished as both a reminder of her beginnings and a charm against failure, yet something no one else seemed to remember but her. A simple pattern of cable and lace worked in a muted blend of grays and yellow, colors that felt like her own quiet signature. Wearing it was her reminder of all she had achieved and how easily it could all vanish.

That scarf, softened with age, was more than a reminder of her skill. It was a talisman of sorts, a piece of her long journey through the ups and downs of a design career that, after more than a decade, was finally finding acclaim. Yet, the thrill of success brought an almost equal measure of dread. Each stitch in that scarf felt like a safeguard against the fear of a sudden loss of it all.

As she adjusted the scarf, tucking it close to guard against the cold, she reminded herself of the purpose of this evening and the entire weekend. She was here to do her job. This evening she would speak about her book, but she would keep a cautious distance, each interaction measured, careful not to overstep. Then for the rest of the weekend, she would teach crocheters and knitters how to make sweaters that fit. And that's all. Her career, more than a decade in the making, had finally reached a tipping point. The book was a milestone, but the success she'd worked so hard for felt delicate, as though any wrong move might unravel it.

With a deep breath, Hazel adjusted the handle of her oversized suitcase, packed to the brim with sweater samples, swatches, copies of her book, and workbooks for her classes. She strode through the automatic doors and immediately spotted the black sedan idling at the curb. As she approached, Marcus, the driver, a middle-aged man with close-cropped salt-and-pepper hair and a polite smile, stepped out to greet her.

"Afternoon, Ms. Whitmore," he said, his voice a warm baritone. He was smartly dressed in dark pants, a black overcoat, and polished black shoes.

Hazel nodded, grateful as he took her heavy suitcase and opened the door for her. "Thank you," she replied, sliding into the backseat.

Inside, the car's warmth enveloped her, easing the tension that had coiled in her shoulders. She exhaled slowly, her breath fogged up the cool glass of the window. The retreat was more than a milestone. It was her big moment. This trip, her first book signing and teaching alongside designers she looked up to, still felt surreal.

For years, Hazel had worked quietly. She had built her reputation stitch by stitch, collaborating with yarn companies and self-publishing designs. Now, shop owners and event organizers took notice and had reached out to her. They wanted her at their events. And here she was, as an honored guest, en route to her first major event. Her right hand instinctively drifted to the back of her left hand, still bruised from where she'd pinched herself earlier. This was really happening.

It only took ten years of hard work to become an overnight success, she thought wryly, her lips curving into a small smile.

As the sedan pulled away from the curb, the airport fading into the distance, they joined the stream of city traffic. Hazel gazed out the window at the cityscape, watching the scenery flash by, buildings and trees blurring together. She clutched her scarf, feeling the familiar texture beneath her fingertips. It reminded her that every stitch she'd made, every step she'd taken had led her to this moment. The weekend would be amazing. She had to believe that.

Chapter 2: Thursday Early-Afternoon

Being in a new city was exciting. As the skyscrapers gave way to open spaces and trees, the car moved toward the outskirts of St. Louis. With each passing mile, they drew closer to the shop, and the retreat schedule ran through Hazel's mind on a loop. She mentally checked off all the events she needed to attend over the weekend: classes to teach, a book signing tonight, a free day for the retreat attendees to shop, and an expectation for teachers to be available to assist students with purchases. Every event had its own demands, and she needed to be prepared for all of it.

But first, she'd be stopping at Yarn-monious. Meeting the staff and getting familiar with the space before the event was part of her preparations, ensuring everything was set up to her liking ahead of the book signing.

For fiber artists, the name alone was legendary.

Hazel had heard about it for years—the Midwest's finest yarn and fiber shop, renowned not just for its sumptuous selection of yarns and notions but for the deep sense of community it fostered. The shop was a haven where crocheters, knitters, spinners, and weavers found not just materials but connection. At its heart was Shanice Keller, a vibrant force of nature whose journey from '90s R&B stardom as a member of the girl group InHarmony to beloved local yarn shop owner added an irresistible layer of charm.

Hazel couldn't wait to experience it in real life: the walls lined with endless skeins of yarn, cozy nooks for stitching, and that distinct, familiar wooly smell that felt like home. The thought filled her with a mixture of excitement and nerves.

Her phone buzzed again. This time, it was a message from Shanice: *Can't wait to meet you, Hazel! Everything is ready on our end for your pre-signing tour. See you soon!*

A smile tugged at Hazel's lips as she read the message. She'd only exchanged a few emails with Shanice, but the woman's warm, effusive, and clear passion for her shop had been impossible to miss. Yet, something about those brief interactions left Hazel with the distinct impression that there was more to Shanice's story than met the eye.

As the car turned the corner and pulled up to the shop, Hazel's breath caught and her heart quickened. Trees flanked the sidewalk, their branches dappled with autumn's fiery hues. Overflowing hanging baskets spilled vibrant fall flowers over their edges, and planters brimming with cheerful mums below lined the storefronts.

The street itself felt like stepping into a postcard. Quaint shops and cafés lined the avenue, their colorful awnings and vintage signage forming a vibrant patchwork of textures and tones. Weathered brick storefronts nestled alongside freshly painted exteriors, an artful blend of history and renewal. Black iron lamp posts, with their timeless design, stood like quiet sentinels along the sidewalk. Wooden benches rested under the shade of sprawling trees, inviting passersby to pause and savor the scene.

Nestled midway along the bustling stretch of brick-lined High Street, Yarn-monious stood out like a whimsical beacon. The shopfront exuded charm, its playful spirit impossible to ignore. The two large bay windows on either side of the front door were framed by ivy-draped trellises showcasing an enticing array of handmade creations. The inviting window display featured colorful granny squares strung together hanging from crochet chains like bunting, chunky wool blankets that looked like they were finger-knitted begged to be touched, hand-knit sweaters, including samples from Hazel's own book, and a rainbow of yarns artfully arranged in baskets.

Above the deep teal door, a hand-carved rustic wooden sign in the shape of a skein of yarn swung gently in the breeze. The words etched into it read: *Yarn-monious—Where Crafting Souls Find Their Rhythm.* Hazel couldn't help but smile at the nod to Shanice's musical past.

"We're here!" Marcus announced, a hint of encouragement in his tone as he exited the driver door.

"You've got this," Hazel whispered under her breath, clutching her bag a little tighter.

Marcus walked around to open her door. "I'll wait for you in the Municipal Parking Lot at the end of the street. Text me when you're ready and I'll take you to your hotel."

"Thank you, Marcus," Hazel replied.

Gathering her handbag and laptop bag, she paused for just a moment before stepping out of the car into the crisp air. She took a steadying breath and tugged her scarf a little tighter around her neck and adjusted the strap of her bag. This was it.

Marcus closed the door and stood waiting for Hazel to enter the shop. Her eyes swept over the shop's exterior. Through the window, she saw a burst of color, rows and rows of yarn in every shade imaginable, like an artist's palette come to life. That familiar excitement bubble up inside her, the itch to dive in, touch everything, and get lost in the texture of it all.

Just as Hazel approached, the shop door swung open. A bell above the door tinkled a cheerful and familiar melody she couldn't quite place. And there she was, Shanice Keller, the owner herself.

Shanice was a vision of effortless grace, the kind of presence that made people stop in their tracks and take notice. Tall and poised, her elegant stature radiated confidence. Her storm-gray eyes sparkled with warmth, contrasting beautifully against her deep brown skin, which seemed to glow in the soft afternoon light.

Long, silver-streaked bohemian braids were piled high on her head, wrapped in a scarf adorned with tiny, crocheted flowers, adding delicate pops of color. A few soft tendrils escaped, framing her striking yet kind face.

She wore a flowing tunic of burnt orange and gold, reminiscent of autumn leaves, paired with sleek black pants and ankle boots that hinted at her knack for blending bohemian charm with modern sophistication. Around her neck, a chunky necklace made of crocheted and beaded strands showcased her love of fiber arts, perfectly illustrating her creative spirit. Shanice exuded a natural authority, tempered by an approachable and easygoing energy.

"Hazel! Welcome!" Shanice greeted warmly, her voice rich and inviting, though edged with a faint nervousness, as if she had been looking forward to this moment just as much.

As Hazel stepped into the shop, she was enveloped by the scent of wool and lavender. The familiar warmth wrapped around her like a comforting embrace. She extended her hand with a polite smile on her face.

For a brief moment, Shanice hesitated, her gaze dropped to Hazel's hand as if uncertain about its meaning. Hazel's confidence faltered, and she began to pull her hand back, wondering if she had misstepped. But then Shanice's expression softened. With a radiant smile, she closed the gap between them and pulled Hazel into a quick heartfelt hug. The embrace was brief but meaningful. Hazel caught a whiff of Shanice's delicate, flowery perfume, a scent that felt almost at odds with the tension radiating from her. Beneath Shanice's warm exterior, there seemed to be a hidden strain, as if she were carrying the weight of the world on her shoulders.

"It's such a pleasure to finally meet you in person. Your work is incredible. We have several of your sweater samples on display, as you may have noticed in the window. Our customers are obsessed with your designs," Shanice said, her enthusiasm evident.

Hazel felt her cheeks heat up. "Thank you so much for having me and for saying that."

Her eyes wandered around the room, taking in the shop's charm. It was even more enchanting than the photos online had suggested. Tabletops were piled high with notions and accessories. Floor-to-ceiling shelves lined every wall, crammed with skeins of yarn in every imaginable color, from the deepest indigo to the softest pastel pink. Each skein seemed to glow, lit by the soft daylight streaming through the tall windows, casting a warm golden hue over the store. Every color and texture called to her, but there was something unspoken simmering just beneath the surface.

In the center of the store, a long wooden table surrounded by chairs was clearly meant for classes and communal gatherings. Nearby, a cozy nook beckoned with a loveseat and two oversized armchairs, their upholstery worn just enough to hint at years of use. Fluffy pillows perched on the seats, and colorful granny-stitch blankets draped casually over the backs, inviting visitors to sink in and stay a while.

Comfortable armchairs were scattered throughout the shop in small, inviting clusters, perfect for crocheters and knitters to pause, needles or hooks in hand, and lose themselves in their craft. The scent of wool mingled gently in the air, and the faint hum of quiet conversation made the space feel alive and welcoming. It was a paradise for fiber artists.

It was not just a shop. It was a fiber artist's dream come to life, a haven where creativity flourished in every corner.

"Shanice, this place is...it's everything I imagined and more." Hazel said, taking it all in.

"Thank you," Shanice replied, a wide smile breaking through. She brushed a strand of her bohemian braids away from her face, "I'm so glad you could make it. How was your flight? I've been looking forward to this for weeks. Come in. There's so much I want to show you before things get too busy later. The retreat, the trunk show... they're going to be amazing. You're going to love it."

Her voice brimmed with excitement but held an edge of anxiousness, almost as if she was trying to convince herself as much as Hazel. "Let me give you the five-cent tour," she said, finally pausing to take a breath.

Shanice led the way, moving gracefully as she navigated the aisles with a sense of ownership and pride. As they strolled through the shop, she pointed out her favorite sections: the hand-dyed yarns from local artisans, the collection of antique knitting needles and crochet hooks displayed in a glass case, and a cozy alcove where skeins of cashmere, alpaca, and silk were lovingly arranged like precious gems, shimmering with an almost magnetic allure.

"This is my little corner of heaven," Shanice said, her voice filled with emotion of all she'd achieved as she gestured around the shop. "I've always wanted a place like this— a sanctuary where people could come together, escape from the hustle and bustle of the outside world, find safety, share their creativity, and feel at home."

Hazel watched her carefully, sensing an undercurrent beneath her words. There was more to the story. "You've created something truly special here," Hazel said sincerely, her gaze sweeping over the inviting space. A note of longing crept into her voice. "I don't have anything like this back at home. I'm almost jealous of all your customers."

Shanice turned to her, curiosity flickering in her eyes. But before she could respond, Hazel redirected the conversation. "How long have you been running the shop?"

Shanice paused, her fingers grazing a skein of deep emerald yarn. Her touch was reverent, as if the yarn carried a memory. "Almost a decade now," she said thoughtfully, her voice tinged with disbelief. "Has it really been that long? It's been quite the journey. Before this, I was... well, let's just say I lived a very different life."

Hazel tilted her head, intrigued. "Different how?" She knew the broad strokes of Shanice's story from online blogs and gossip, but something in Shanice's tone suggested there was more to it.

Shanice chuckled, the sound low and melodic with an edge of wistfulness. "I used to be in the music industry—R&B, to be exact. Back in the nineties, I had a little fame," she admitted, her smile dimming as a shadow crossed her face. "I made some mistakes and got caught up in a lifestyle that just wasn't for me anymore."

Her gaze drifted across the shop, and her voice softened. "I wanted something quieter, something that let me reconnect with myself. Yarn did that for me. It has a way of doing that, you know?"

Hazel nodded, understanding her on a visceral level and marveling at the layers of this woman. "I do. It's amazing how life can lead us to places we never expected." Hazel thought back to her life just a year ago when she struggled to get her design proposal accepted by major publications, and now here she was as the author of a bestselling crochet and knit book.

"Isn't it?" Shanice agreed, her eyes sparkling. "And speaking of the unexpected, let me introduce you to someone."

Chapter 3: Thursday Afternoon

They turned a corner and entered a sunlit nook where a young woman in her mid-twenties lounged in an oversized armchair, her long legs draped casually over the armrest. She was deeply engrossed in crocheting a small, intricate amigurumi figure, which Hazel realized was a musical note, complete with tiny arms and a cheerful face.

"This is my beautiful and brilliant daughter, KNote, and soon to be Dr. Keller. She's completing her PhD in Social Work," Shanice said, beaming with motherly pride. She turned to her daughter. "KNote," Shanice added, her voice blending affection and exasperation, "say hello to Hazel. She's the designer I've been raving about."

KNote glanced up, her dark skin glowing and her midnight eyes narrowing slightly as she assessed Hazel.

"Hey," KNote greeted, her tone cool but polite. She swung her legs over the side of the chair and planted her sneaker-clad feet on the floor. Setting her crochet hook down on a side table, she held up the nearly finished amigurumi with both hands, her expression a mix of pride and nonchalance. "What do you think?" she asked, not fishing for approval. She was confident in her work.

Her hair, styled in waist-length box braids adorned with golden cuffs, framed a strikingly beautiful face, though her expression was guarded. She wore a cropped crochet sweater that revealed a sliver of toned stomach, paired with high-waisted jeans and pristine sneakers that looked as if they had never touched a grimy sidewalk. Hazel thought she looked surprisingly young for all she's accomplished.

Hazel leaned in closer, furrowing her brow slightly as she studied the piece. The stitches were tight and even, and the details were meticulous. "It's fantastic," she said sincerely. "You've got a real talent. What pattern are you following?"

KNote shrugged, a hint of a smile tugging at her lips. "Thanks, but it's not from a pattern. I'm just making it up as I go," she said, turning the amigurumi in her hands to evaluate it. Satisfied, she picked up her hook and resumed crocheting.

"I've been working on it for a couple of days," KNote continued, her eyes focused on her work. "Mom keeps bugging me to help out in the shop more, but..." She trailed off, her voice conveying a note of playful defiance.

"KNote," Shanice interjected, mild annoyance threading her voice, "you can crochet *and* help customers when you're not busy with classes. It's not an either-or situation."

Hazel couldn't help but laugh; the dynamic between mother and daughter reminding her of conversations she'd had with her own mother. However, just as quickly as the memories surfaced, she pushed them aside to focus on the present. She didn't want to go down that road...not right now. "It's clear creativity runs in the family," she said, hoping to smooth things over.

Shanice smiled, letting her annoyance melt away. "That it does," she said, rubbing her daughter's shoulder. "Though sometimes I think she takes it for granted."

"Maybe," KNote admitted, "but it's not like you'd survive without me." She winked at Hazel.

"Brat," Shanice teased, playfully slapping KNote's arm, a proud grin lighting up her face.

"I got it from my mama!" KNote shot back in a sing-song voice.

They both laughed, and the sound filled the room, reflecting their bond. It was clear there was a deep connection between them. Shanice rolled her eyes, but her gaze lingered on KNote with unmistakable affection. "Come on, Hazel. Let me show you the rest of the shop. KNote needs to have that finished and in the window on display by the end of the weekend."

Hazel followed Shanice, glancing back at KNote, who was already engrossed in her project again. There was something endearing about KNote's unshakeable confidence, even if it bordered on arrogance. It was evident that she and Shanice had built something special together—something Hazel felt lucky to witness, even if only briefly.

Shanice's glance briefly darted to the back of the shop, and Hazel's eyes followed to where a flurry of activity unfolded. A small team of employees carefully unpacked a vibrant assortment of yarns from boxes. These must be special inventory for the trunk show. Hazel eyed the yarn with eager anticipation, wanting to take a closer look and maybe touch a few skeins.

"Come, let me show you the yarn featured for the retreat," Shanice said, her voice brimming with excitement as she led Hazel to the back room.

Hazel hurried to keep up, as Shanice's longer strides set a brisk pace. As they passed an overstuffed armchair, Shanice grabbed a sweater draped over one arm and casually tossed it over her shoulders. It was clearly a favorite piece, the kind of sweater that felt like a hug on chilly mornings. The sleeves were slightly stretched from years of wear, and the pockets sagged just a bit, heavy with the daily odds and ends they'd held over time. The sweater was a story in itself, embodying countless cozy moments and practical use.

Shanice paused just outside the back room and glanced around. "I wanted to introduce you to my store manager, Jules, but I don't see her," Shanice said, a hint of disappointment in her voice. "You'll meet her later at your book signing."

Around them, employees moved with quiet precision, handling each skein of yarn as though it were a rare artifact. Hazel's fingers itched to reach out and touch the yarn, to let the textures and colors spill through her hands. The dyer's trunk show, a limited-time event showcasing a one-of-a-kind collection, had transformed the shop into a treasure trove. Each skein was imbued with hues so rich they seemed to glow against the rustic wood shelves, reflecting the meticulous work of the dyer's hand.

The air was charged with a quiet buzz of energy, the kind that comes from knowing something special is happening. This wasn't the usual yarn stocked on the shelves. It was a unique showcase that gave attendees a rare chance to purchase yarns unavailable anywhere else.

Shanice's presence, both grounded and lively, seemed to amplify the atmosphere, infusing the bustling scene with energy and anticipation. Her excitement rippled through the room, setting a tone of creativity and expectation. However, as Hazel studied Shanice, she couldn't shake the feeling that her bright demeanor was slightly forced, her gaze flicking to the back room too often.

After a moment, Shanice continued the tour. They walked over to another yarn display, and Hazel picked up a skein.

"The yarn selection is absolutely stunning," Hazel said sincerely as she admired a skein of deep-blue worsted weight superwash merino wool. It shimmered subtly in the light, the color impossibly rich. "This is another specialty colorway for the trunk show, right?"

Shanice nodded, her enthusiasm returning. "Yes! The dyer is Sunset Fiber Works. Gorgeous, right? Are you familiar with them?"

"Not very well," Hazel admitted.

"Okay, let me tell you," Shanice said, her voice rising with excitement. "They are a mother-daughter dyeing duo based here in Missouri, about an hour north. They're Verna and Shameka Shales. They've only been dyeing yarn professionally for eighteen months, but they've already established themselves as the queen and princess of color. They've even recently expanded to dye spinning fiber and create glass-blown drop spindles. Each drop spindle is handmade and one-of-a-kind; no two are alike," Shanice explained. While her tone was enthusiastic, her smile didn't quite reach her eyes. "We're excited to be the only shop carrying their new products, especially the drop spindles."

"That's incredible," Hazel said, making a mental note. As a designer, she was always on the lookout for dyers to collaborate on new projects, especially those who were not yet well known. This was one she'd love to get to know better.

Hazel picked up another skein of yarn, this one in a variegated earth-toned colorway. She read the fiber content and how many yards and meters were in each skein, mentally calculating what she could make with one skein and how many she'd need for a sweater.

"The duo was expected to be here this weekend for the trunk show to talk about their yarn, their dyeing process, inspiration, and answer questions," Shanice continued, her voice faltering slightly. "But at the last minute, they, um..." She paused, seemingly searching for the right words. "They decided they couldn't make the journey down," she finished, almost relieved. She tapped her fingers rhythmically on the edge of the display, as if she were keeping time with a song only she could hear.

Hazel glanced at Shanice, sensing the underlying tension again. She put the skein back and pulled out her phone. "Mind if I take a few pictures of the shop and all you have to offer for my blog and socials?"

"Not at all, go ahead," Shanice replied. "The new fibers and drop spindles by Sunset Fiber Works are over there," she pointed at a section dedicated to spinning. Hazel glanced over and was immediately in awe. There were several spinning wheels in various models and designs, all ready for use. Although Hazel was not yet a spinner, the process fascinated her. The idea of turning wool fluff into yarn and then using that yarn to create a sweater was next on her fiber bucket list.

"Thanks for the tour, Shanice," Hazel said, barely taking her eyes off the array of spinning tools.

Shanice nodded absentmindedly and hurried to the back of the shop, throwing instructions to one of her employees over her shoulder.

Chapter 4: Thursday Afternoon

Hazel snapped a few photos, capturing the rich hues and the cozy vibe of the shop. She was drawn to the spinning area, which featured colorful fibers displayed in vibrant piles alongside a selection of masterfully crafted spinning wheels and drop spindles, both handmade and commercially produced.

On a nearby table, drop spindles of various sizes and designs stood in neat rows. Hazel picked up a striking blue glass-blown drop spindle adorned with yellow and white swirls that gleamed under the shop lights. She turned it around in her hand, testing the weight and balance. It felt delicate yet sturdy. Hazel noticed the tag attached to the hook at the top of the wooden shaft, which reads 'Sunset Fiber Works'. This must be one of their new products.

"Gorgeous," she murmured, gently rotating the glass drop spindle between her fingers. The whorl was delicate yet well-crafted, while the sturdy shaft, made of solid hardwood, balanced it perfectly. The sterling silver hook gleamed under the light. "I really should try my hand at drop spindling someday," she said aloud, though she wasn't speaking to anyone in particular. Carefully, she returned the drop spindle to its spot and moved on to another table filled with knitting notions, handmade polymer buttons, and an array of project bags in cheeky quotes. She took more photos, knowing that later, she would write a blog post to recap the day, and these images would add to the story.

As she studied the shop's displays, a young woman of average height with a shaved head and a lavender knit scarf tied around her neck approached, her arms filled with skeins of yarn. She stopped in front of Hazel.

"Wait. It's you," she said breathlessly. "You're Hazel Whitmore! I love your book," she exclaimed. "I'm Jenika Steveson, full-time yarn wrangler and part-time student." A wide grin spread across her face, showcasing white teeth against her dark skin.

Jenika stood close enough for Hazel to spot the edge of a rose tattoo on her neck, emerging from under the scarf. She shifted the yarn in her arms to offer a handshake. A simple tattoo reading '11:11' peeked out from underneath her sleeve on the inside of her wrist.

Hazel had always wanted a tattoo but had been too scared. What if she chose something and then she didn't like it anymore? What would its meaning become? What would people think of her? These were the thoughts that kept her from taking that leap.

"Thank you! I was trying to *not* get a big head this weekend. You're not helping," Hazel chuckled awkwardly, shaking Jenika's offered hand. "Nice to meet you, Jenika. How long have you been working here?"

"Almost six months now," Jenika said. Her eyes were so dark her pupils blended in, sparkling as she played with the tail of the scarf. "I love it. The yarn community here is so vibrant and diverse, though it's been a little...chaotic today." A slight frown creased her smooth forehead, and her eyes seemed to lose their shine. Jenika's brief hesitation hadn't gone unnoticed.

She quickly turned on the smile retailers held in reserve for customers, a detached smile that didn't quite reach her eyes. It was a smile Hazel knew all too well from her days working in retail.

Hazel nodded. "I can imagine," she said, glancing in Shanice's direction, who was animatedly speaking with lots of hand gestures.

Jenika followed Hazel's gaze to land on Shanice, her smile faltering slightly before she glanced at the display that Hazel had photographed.

"Yeah, retreat prep. Everything needs to go perfectly." She laughed nervously but didn't elaborate. "Nice meeting you, and I'll see you later," she said and returned to stocking the retreat yarn on the tabletops.

Hazel wandered through the aisles a bit longer, admiring the shop's offerings and taking photos and videos to share later with her social media followers. However, she couldn't shake the feeling that something was amiss. The warm, cozy atmosphere clashed with the palpable tension hanging in the air. What was going on here? Was it simply anxiety about the retreat, the teachers, and the attendees? Or was it something deeper?

Hazel made her way back to the table filled with the trunk show yarn. Shanice was adding more yarn but she had seemed distracted, almost jittery. Hazel watched Shanice's hands move quickly, the tension in the air becoming unmistakable. Shanice's eyes kept flicking toward the back room, her attention clearly divided, as though she was expecting someone or waiting for something to happen.

Hazel shifted her weight, holding her bag tightly against her side. She felt the prickling sensation of being an outsider, as if her presence was more of a burden than a welcome. She squeezed her woolen scarf, feeling the familiar pull of anxiety she had come to associate with these events. Was there something going on with the shop?

Hazel cleared her throat softly, hoping to break the unspoken awkwardness. "Shanice," she said, keeping her tone light, "was there anything else you needed to go over with me for this evening's book signing before I head over to my hotel to freshen up?"

Shanice glanced up, startled, as if just realizing Hazel was standing there. She quickly offered a thin smile that didn't quite reach her eyes. "Oh! Right...the signing," she said, sounding distracted. "No, I think we're all set for tonight," she replied, her hands still busy adjusting skeins of yarn without really looking at them. "There! That's the last skein," she said, her hands trembling as she stroked a few of the skeins.

Noticing Hazel watching her hands, Shanice quickly tucked her hands in the pockets of her sweater.

"Let's finish your tour to show you where you'll be signing tonight," Shanice said, overly cheerful as she chatted about the evening's events. "The display's all set up, and we've got plenty of copies of your book. I'll make sure the space is ready with water, sweater samples, and swatches by the time you're back later."

"Great," Hazel replied, forcing a polite smile as she tried to shake off the lingering feeling of being in the way. She tightened her grip on her bag and glanced around the shop again, hoping her expression didn't betray the slight disappointment settling in her chest. She had expected a warm welcome and maybe even some camaraderie, but instead, she was left feeling like she had walked into a situation she wasn't supposed to be part of.

She quickly messaged Marcus to let him know she was ready to go.

Shanice's gaze had already drifted back to the back room. Hazel turned and started to walk toward the front door, with Shanice following her. She tucked her scarf a little tighter around her neck, hoping the cool air outside would feel more welcoming than the tension-filled warmth inside Yarn-monious.

"Everything looks amazing. See you tonight," Hazel said softly as she walked out the door, her voice almost lost underneath the musical notes of the door chime.

"See you later," Shanice replied with a small wave.

Outside, the autumn sun was fading, and the brisk air hit Hazel's cheeks. She exhaled, feeling the weight lift slightly as the door closed behind her. She felt a pang of disappointment settled in her chest. This retreat was her first big event since the book release, and she had been looking forward to it for months. She had imagined this moment going differently, perhaps warmer. Was she expecting too much? This was a big event for them too, after all. But as she glanced back, she saw Shanice already turned away, focused on something out of sight. A hint of doubt lingered, mixing with the chill in the air as Hazel waited for her ride.

Something wasn't right.

Chapter 5: Thursday Afternoon

The ride to the hotel was quicker than Hazel had anticipated. The gentle hum of the engine and the rhythm of the passing scenery lulled her into a light sleep. She jolted awake when the car pulled under the portico and snapped her head up. A yawn escaped her as she rubbed one bleary eye, trying to shake off the fog.

Marcus opened her car door with practiced efficiency. "Go on inside," he said with a warm smile. "I'll grab your bags from the trunk and bring them to the lobby."

"Thank you, Marcus," Hazel replied softly.

As she stepped out of the car, the crisp autumn air instantly revived her. She smoothed the front of her trench coat, taking a moment to pull it snug against the chill. Glancing around, the grandeur of the hotel came into full focus.

The hotel's automatic doors slid open with a soft whoosh and she stepped inside, immediately struck by the bustling energy of the lobby. Laughter bubbled from a corner, mingling with the faint hum of conversations and the occasional ding of an elevator. The high ceilings made the space feel expansive, while a massive chandelier of intertwined glass strands refracted the afternoon sunlight, casting shimmering rainbows across the room.

Clusters of modern furniture arranged in seating areas beckoned guests to linger, and the faint aroma of fresh coffee hinted at a nearby café or coffee station. Hazel's gaze instinctively followed the laughter to its source, where a group of retreat teachers gathered near a cluster of armchairs.

At the center of the group stood Selene Hopkins, effortlessly commanding attention.

Selene was tall and statuesque, her skin glowing under the chandelier's light. Her dark eyes sparkled with an intensity that could warm or scorch, depending on her mood. Tight curls framed her face, perfectly styled as though she'd just stepped out of a photoshoot. She wore a tailored emerald jumpsuit that moved like water when she gestured, paired with her signature asymmetrical oversize shawl draped effortlessly across one shoulder.

Hazel's mind flashed back to high school. Back then, she had been the dorky kid with braces who didn't fit into the clique. Watching Selene, surrounded by her adoring group brought back that feeling of being an outsider, the awkward girl trying not to shrink into the shadows. The memory of stifled laughter at her expense and whispered jokes she wasn't privy to pressed down on her chest like a lead weight.

Hazel hesitated, her pulse quickening.

Selene Hopkins. A name that once inspired admiration now carried a sting that Hazel couldn't quite shake. Years ago, when Hazel was still full of hope for her burgeoning career, she had nervously composed an email to Selene, seeking advice about landing a book deal. The response had been curt and dismissive: *"Do your own research. Stop looking for handouts."*

Had she been looking for a handout? The question still haunted Hazel at times, a quiet echo she couldn't quite silence. The words had felt like a slap to the face, stinging more than she cared to admit. It wasn't just the rejection. It was the dismissiveness from someone she had respected. Yet those words also ignited a fire within her. That moment served as a harsh lesson, solidifying Hazel's resolve to forge her own path and become the support for others that she hadn't received.

Still, standing here now, her chest tightened as the memory resurfaced. She'd known Selene would be teaching at the retreat, but she hadn't anticipated seeing her just yet. She hadn't had time to prepare. Adjusting her purse, she turned toward the front desk, hoping to avoid any interaction altogether. But Selene's voice pierced through the air like an arrow.

"Yo-ho, Hazel!"

Hazel froze. No, no, no, not yet.

"Hazel," came the voice again.

Taking a deep breath, Hazel pasted a polite smile on her face before turning toward the group.

Selene waved her over with exaggerated enthusiasm. "Come. Join us!"

Hazel glanced at Marcus, who had just wheeled her luggage into the lobby, then at the front desk clerk, as if to convey she was busy. But Selene either didn't notice or didn't care.

"Come, come!" Selene called again, her wave growing even more animated.

Hazel sighed softly, giving Marcus an apologetic glance. "Thank you, Marcus," she said quietly, a hint of exasperation in her tone.

"You're welcome." Marcus replied with a wink, his expression warm with reassurance. "I'll be back later to take you to the yarn shop for your book signing."

Grateful for his steady presence, Hazel straightened her posture, channeling her confident alter ego, Whitley. Her steps felt heavier with each one she took toward the group, but she forced herself forward, her expression calm and composed.

"Hello, everyone. Selene. It's so good to see you all," Hazel said, her voice cool and steady despite the knot tightening in her chest.

"We were just catching up," Selene said, offering a dazzling smile that didn't reach her eyes. She turned slightly, ensuring everyone in the group remained focused on her. "The teachers have decided to go to dinner together tonight." She tilted her head slightly, her words carried a hint of condescension. "You should come, too. I know you're new to the scene, but it would be great for you to be around more experienced designers and teachers."

The smile Selene offered Hazel was syrupy sweet, but her tone was sharp enough to cut.

Hazel's cheeks burned. Around her, the group remained silent, their expressions either politely neutral or cautiously disengaged. Some avoided her gaze entirely, while others nodded along with Selene's suggestion like a line of bobblehead dolls.

"Thanks for the invite, Selene," Hazel replied, her voice even. "But I'll have to decline. I have my book signing and talk at the yarn shop around dinner time. And after a long flight, I'm not sure I'd be great company. Maybe another time."

Before Selene could respond, Hazel turned to the group with a small smile. "I hope you all enjoy your dinner."

With that, she walked to the front desk, feeling Selene's eyes on her back the entire way.

The check-in process was mercifully quick, and soon Hazel was dragging her suitcase into the elevator. She quickly found her room and entered her sanctuary.

As the door clicked shut behind her, Hazel leaned against it, exhaling a heavy sigh. She could feel the tension from the encounter still clinging to her, and for a moment, her resolve wavered.

"This is what it's always been like," she muttered to herself. "Always on the outside looking in."

A single tear slid down her cheek, but she wiped it away quickly. "You got this," she whispered, repeating the words until they began to feel true.

After a moment, she pushed herself off the door and surveyed the room. It was a spacious suite with a kitchenette and a cozy sitting area—perfect. Further into the room was a loveseat and a TV mounted on a wall. Around the corner was a king-size bed with an ensuite bathroom. She could already picture herself spreading out her workbooks, sweater samples, and swatches to prepare for each day's events.

Her journey hadn't been quick or easy, but it was her own, and for that, she felt grateful. Occasionally, she wished she had achieved success sooner, but if she was honest with herself, the timing of her rise felt just right, considering everything she had to offer her readers. She needed her struggles and experiences to connect with them, and she wouldn't trade that for anything.

Chapter 6: Thursday Evening

Hazel arrived at the yarn shop precisely at the time Shanice suggested. Since checking into her hotel, where a welcoming gift basket filled with chocolates, teas, and retreat yarns awaited her, along with a note from Shanice, the day's buoyant energy had eased her earlier anxieties about the weekend. The thoughtful gesture soothed the lingering uncertainty she had felt. Perhaps any tension with Shanice earlier was simply pre-event nerves.

Carefully dressed in the most popular sweater from her book, paired with a simple black dress, ankle boots, and her signature scarf, Hazel checked her phone. It was 5:58 p.m., two minutes early—just the right amount of time. As an introvert, she preferred not to arrive too early and risk awkward small talk; however, the anxiety of being late was equally unappealing.

Taking a deep breath, Hazel summoned her alter ego, the brave and confident Whitley, and stepped into the yarn shop. The bell above the entrance chimed its familiar, lilting melody. The air inside the cozy haven was a warm contrast to the biting cold outside. It was filled with the familiar earthy scent of wool, and evening light filtered through shelves stacked with yarns in every hue. The buzz of voices layered over her quiet pep talk. "Come on, girl, you got this." She repeated the mantra inwardly with each step. "Whitley is right here with you. Just like all the practice runs. You're here to inspire."

Shanice waited at the entrance, greeting Hazel with a bright smile. "Hazel, you're here!" Shanice exclaimed, wrapping an arm around Hazel's shoulder. "Welcome to your book signing!" The taller woman paused, obviously proud as she took in the scene. The room was completely transformed from earlier. The large table in the middle had been replaced with smaller tables laden with trays of canapes, water bottles, and glasses of wine.

The shop buzzed with lively conversations and laughter, far beyond what Hazel had anticipated for her first book signing. Groups of people clustered together, some nibbling on plates of cheese and fruit, others admiring yarn from the trunk show, while a few tested out various notions on display. Shanice linked arms with Hazel, guiding her warmly through the bustling crowd toward the signing area.

In the background, music from Shanice's solo ballad album filled the room, setting the mood of the evening. Hazel smiled as memories flooded back when the familiar chords from "Eleven-Eleven" her favorite track on the *Make A Wish* album drifted through the air. The song had once been her anchor, playing on a loop during nights when her dreams felt too far away. It was her lifeline, a whispered nudge from the universe to keep going and pursue a vision she couldn't let go.

As Hazel's gaze shifted to Shanice, the weight of Shanice's celebrity struck her for the first time. This wasn't just a collaborator; it was *Shanice*. A woman whose life had been extraordinary and larger-than-life. Hazel marveled at the thought of such a remarkable journey, the realization washing over her with quiet awe.

People milled around in groups, talking, sipping wine, and enjoying delicious-looking finger foods. "The whole shop's buzzing about meeting the author behind the sweaters everyone's been raving about," Shanice said, waving a hand to gesture at the gathered crowd, her voice rising warmly above the chatter. "Get ready for a night to remember."

Hazel looked around the room, wide-eyed and amazed at the turnout. She'd expected interest in the book, but actually being there and seeing all these crocheters and knitters, everyone here to see her and hear her talk about the book and sign their copies, was beyond anything she could have imagined.

Writing this book was never something Hazel had planned. It all happened by accident. On a whim, she created a sweater and wrote a blog post about how she had adjusted the standard body measurements that many designers used to create sweaters to fit her own body. She demonstrated how she used her own body measurements along with those from her favorite store-bought sweaters to create a template for her perfect fit. That post went viral.

She leveraged that interest to write more sweater patterns, showing how others could do the same, and self-published the book. Less than six months later, a publisher reached out to acquire it. A year later, here she was, at a book signing in one of the largest yarn shops in the country.

Shanice's eyes sparkled as she admired Hazel's outfit. "You look amazing by the way. This is your *Love Yourself Pullover*, right? It looks absolutely stunning on you. It's the top pattern our customers are coming in for yarn to make. It's an absolute hit," Shanice exclaimed. "I can't tell you how thrilled everyone is that you are here," she added, glancing around at the large turnout.

It had been a whirlwind year, but Hazel couldn't help the spark of excitement that flared in her chest at how much she had achieved. Months after the launch of her book, *Sweaters That Fit*, she was finally here, sharing everything she knew to help crocheters and knitters make sweaters that actually fit.

"Thank you, Shanice! You and your team have created something fantastic here," Hazel replied, feeling the weight of lingering doubt lift as Shanice gave her arm a friendly squeeze.

As they made their way through the crowd toward the signing area, they passed a woman holding two skeins of yarn up and scrutinizing them closely. The woman, who looked vaguely familiar but whom Hazel couldn't quite place, appeared frustrated as she replaced the skeins on the pile, as if they were hot to the touch. She picked up another skein, flipped it to read the back for the ball band, and replaced it as well. She repeated this process with two more skeins, twisting them this way and that to examine them. She frowned slightly and mumbled, "That's the price they're selling these for? Unbelievable," loud enough for those nearby to hear.

Hazel had heard too many complaints about prices of yarn and patterns, as though the creators were getting rich from them. Some people even claimed, rather loudly, they could get the same yarn at a big box store or similar patterns for free on dubious websites. So much effort goes into creating these items that the creators deserve to be fairly compensated for their work. It was a conversation worth having every time she encountered it. Hazel had even had the pleasure of correcting people in the past, but today she decided to ignore the woman, her focus drawn to the inviting setup of the signing area at the back of the shop.

The corner had been transformed into a presentation space, complete with rows of chairs framed by shelves of vibrant skeins and softly lit lamps, giving it an intimate and inviting feel. A small stack of her books sat beside a vase of pink roses, her favorite flowers, adding a personal touch. Already, knitters, crocheters, and yarn enthusiasts were seated, chatting and leafing through their copies.

"I'll be right back," Shanice said, leaving Hazel standing alone at the edge of the signing area.

A short, curvy woman with short auburn curls hurried over. She appeared to be in her thirties, dressed in black pants, sensible shoes, and an oversized knit pullover that made her almost blend in, rendering her unnoticeable. Her features were plain and unremarkable. "Hi, Hazel.

I'm Jules Bustamante, the store manager. We've been communicating via email to set this up," she reminded Hazel, her voice coming out in a rush. "Sorry I missed your visit earlier."

Hazel shook Jules' offered hand. "Thank you, Jules. It's so nice to meet you in person and put a face to an email."

"If you need anything while you're in town, don't hesitate to let me know," Jules replied, then rushed away as quickly as she'd come. With such a big event going on, she was busy buzzing around the room, cleaning up spills and making sure everything was in order.

Hazel positioned herself at the front of the room and took a moment to look out at the attendees, reflecting on this historic moment in her long and challenging career. She silently recalled her journey and all the times when she felt like quitting. Thankfully, she had stuck with it, as all her hard work had *finally* paid off.

After a few minutes, holding a glass of red wine in one hand, Shanice approached the front of the room to call everyone to order. Hazel stood to the side, nervously wringing her hands together behind her. "Just breathe," she reminded herself under her breath. Everyone quieted as they found places to sit or stand at the back.

"Welcome, everyone, to tonight's book signing event with the illustrious designer and author, Hazel Whitmore. Hazel has been designing crochet and knit patterns for over a decade. Her recent book is one that is close to my heart as a fluffy woman." Shanice chuckled, picking up a copy of the book and holding it up for everyone to see. She flipped it over and read the back cover, "According to the back blurb, Hazel says 'This book is my love letter to the people who don't fit the mold and don't see themselves represented. It's for anyone who doesn't feel seen. I see you! You're worthy.' So let's put our happy Yarn-monious hands together and welcome our special guest, Hazel Whitmore," she finished with a sweeping gesture toward Hazel.

Shanice raised her glass of wine in Hazel's direction and whispered, "Cheers!" She took a sip, scrunched her face in confusion, and looked into her glass. "This bottle has gone bad," she said offhandedly to herself before walking away and leaving Hazel alone.

Hazel had never envisioned herself standing in front of a room full of people, let alone being the center of attention. She had always thrived behind the scenes, content to let her creativity speak for itself. The shadows felt safe, predictable, and comforting, her refuge from the glaring spotlight. But the book had turned her world upside down, thrusting her into a role she hadn't asked for and certainly wasn't prepared to play.

Everything had happened so fast. One moment, she was pouring over measurements and stitch counts at her kitchen table, and the next, her inbox was flooded with interview requests, invitations to events, and messages from readers who saw her as a trailblazer. Fame wasn't something she actively sought out; it had arrived unannounced, like a summer storm, sweeping away her carefully constructed anonymity before she had a chance to brace herself.

She hadn't had time to prepare, let alone process the shift. One day, she was Hazel-the-quiet-designer who blogged about her struggles to find patterns that fit her body. Now, she was Hazel-the-author, with her face on websites and strangers lining up to meet her. Yet, here she was, standing at the front of the room, every pair of eyes locked on her, waiting for her to say something meaningful. Her hands felt clammy, her pulse raced, and for a split second, she considered running. But then she caught sight of a woman in the audience, clutching a copy of her book to her chest as if it were a lifeline.

That's when it hit her: this wasn't about fame, fear, or even herself. It was about connection. It was about providing a resource to a sector of the fiber community that had always been left out.

With a steadying breath, Hazel launched into her rehearsed talk. She began by sharing her design journey, discussing the inspiration behind her book, her struggles with body image from childhood into adulthood, and why it was so essential to write patterns celebrating every body, shape, and size. Her words flowed as she spoke of inclusivity and her deep desire for all who loved knitting and crocheting to feel valued and seen. As she glanced around, she noticed heads nodding in agreement, and her confidence solidified.

When she invited questions, hands shot up instantly. One of the first was from a woman in a wheelchair at the front, who raised her hand with a shy smile. Her voice, though soft, held resolve. "I've been knitting for years, but since my accident two years ago, fitting patterns to my body has been a challenge," she said, glancing at her upper arms. "Wheeling myself around has built more muscle here, and it's been hard to find a pattern that fits my changing body. I am learning to appreciate all my body has done for me without losing the style I love."

Hazel's heart warmed. Hearing stories like this validated every late night and anxious moment she had poured into her work. "Thank you for sharing that...," she paused to glance at the woman's name tag, "...Melinda," she replied, her voice gentle, yet strong. "I love that you've found ways to stay connected to knitting. Adjusting the fit isn't always simple, but with the right tweaks and adjustments, you can definitely make a piece that honors both your style and needs."

Diving in, Hazel shared tips for adjusting sleeve measurements, encouraging experimenting with swatches to explore potential modifications, and suggested hemming tops to avoid tangling with wheelchair wheels. As she spoke, Melinda's face lit up with a blend of enthusiasm and relief.

"Thank you, Hazel. Those are brilliant suggestions I hadn't thought about before. I really appreciate your insight," she said.

Hazel nodded gratefully at Melinda. This is why I do this, she thought, for these moments when just one person leaves feeling, seen, valued, and understood. The spark in Melinda's eyes as she described her love for knitting and her newfound appreciation for her changing body reminded Hazel why all her self-doubt had been worth it.

Another hand shot up in the back. "Yes, what's your question?" Hazel asked, gesturing to the tall figure with large bantu knots and flawless skin.

"Thank you, Hazel, for taking my question," they said. "My name is Wren, and I believe I speak for all of us when I say we appreciate the resource you've created for us," they added, glancing around the room.

Hazel placed a hand on her chest in gratitude, noticing heads nodding in agreement. While she was thankful, it was also embarrassing to hear such praise; she wished they would skip the compliments and ask their questions. But that wasn't how this worked. She stood there awkwardly, her cheeks warming, with a wide smile fixed on her face and her heart pounding with every word. She often wondered if her reaction was appropriate for the situation.

"I have more of a statement rather than a question. As a non-binary person, I used to struggle with sweater patterns. The patterns were always for either men or women, with fits tailored to those body types; curvy for women and boxy for men. What I loved about your book is that the sweaters were just sweaters. The patterns don't have genders, which made it fun for me because I didn't have to choose. I could just be me," their voice cracked at the end. They paused to take a couple of deep breaths. An older man nearby wrapped a supporting hand around their shoulder. Applause broke out to lend additional strength and support.

Swallowing hard, they continued. "What was your motivation for doing that?"

Hazel didn't know what to say. She was overcome with emotion, just like the rest of the room. "Thank you so much, Wren, for sharing your story with all of us tonight. You didn't have to, but we appreciate it. You deserve cute sweaters too." She paused to applaud Wren, and everyone joined in.

Once the room was quiet again, Hazel said, "My motivation for this book is simple: inclusion. The book is a love letter to myself, to you, and to everyone here who needs it. Plain and simple. I can't make it be about anything else. Is it perfect? Absolutely not. I don't pretend to know everything. I've missed things, and I am always learning. While I can't go back and add everything I want to this book, I'm continuously updating my blog to include more information. This book is a small part of a larger movement that we are all responsible for advancing in our craft. You deserve to be a part of it!"

More hands went up. Hazel settled into the conversation and felt increasingly confident with each question. As the event continued, she found herself fully in her element, chatting with fans who shared stories, brought project notebooks, and eagerly sought her advice. She spoke and offered encouragement until her voice began to fade. After her talk and Q&A session, she signed books, adding personalized notes to inspire and motivate. By the time the last attendee left, she was exhausted but deeply fulfilled.

Tonight was amazing. Hazel was on cloud nine. Nothing could ruin the joy of this evening.

Chapter 7: Thursday Evening

Hazel signed the last book and began to gather her bags, carefully stowing away leftover books and sweater samples. The remaining customers made their final purchases and headed out the door. The Yarn-monious staff worked quickly to restore the room to order, cleaning up the food and wine while tidying the store.

A few minutes passed, and Hazel completed packing up her final items. She glanced around; the shop was empty. She was alone. Grabbing her bags, she walked toward the office, wondering if she was truly alone in the shop. As she got closer, she heard faint voices drifting out of the office, breaking the silence. She caught snippets of conversations—"*It's illegal...,' 'You're going to pay...,' 'Shh, somebody might hear...'*"—before the voices quieted again.

A chill ran down her spine. Hazel paused, her hand stilled on her bag as she glanced in the direction of the voices, tempted to slip out of the shop quietly to avoid getting involved. She didn't want to eavesdrop, but the words sent a shiver through her. *Whatever was happening sounded very serious,* she thought. She turned, planning to leave undetected.

Just then, a floorboard creaked behind her, and Jenika appeared, startling Hazel.

"Oh! You scared me!" Hazel let out a small, nervous laugh, her hand instinctively touching the scarf around her neck.

"Sorry about that," Jenika said with a quick smile. "Got everything?" she asked, looking at Hazel's bags and back at the nook to see if anything had been missed. "Shanice is busy at the moment, and I'm not sure where Jules has gone," she paused to glance around the store to confirm they were alone. "So, I've come to thank you for a fantastic evening and walk you out."

Hazel nodded, glancing toward the back room. "Is everything alright back there?" she asked, keeping her tone casual.

Jenika's smile wavered, a flicker Hazel might have missed had she not been watching closely. "Oh, it's fine!" Jenika replied a bit too quickly, her hand fluttering briefly to her collar as if to loosen an invisible tension. Shifting the conversation, she added, "Everyone had an amazing time. The feedback so far has been off the charts, just as we'd expected."

"That's wonderful to hear," Hazel replied, her mood lightening slightly as her phone vibrated with a message from Marcus, her driver: *I'm outside whenever you're ready.*

"Did you get a chance to meet Verna Shales of Sunset Fiber Works?" Jenika asked as they walked together to the front door.

Confused, Hazel responded, "No, Shanice said they couldn't come down, so I assumed they weren't here. And no one introduced me to them." What was going on? Why hadn't Shanice introduced her, knowing she wanted to discuss a potential collaboration? So many thoughts swirled in her head.

Jenika shrugged. "I don't know why you didn't meet her. You walked right past Verna when you arrived. She was the older woman at the trunk show table."

That's why she looked so familiar. After leaving the shop earlier, Hazel had quickly researched Sunset Fiber Work to learn about who they were and what they stood for. Before any collaboration, Hazel always did her due diligence to ensure her values aligned with the dyer. She hadn't spent much time looking at their headshot photos during her brief reconnaissance. Now she remembered the woman and the anger on her face at the trunk show table. Why was she so upset about the yarn? It couldn't be the price—the dyers determined what to charge. Hazel had so many questions. But was it any of her business? Shaking her head to clear her thoughts, she recognized that she had too much on her plate this weekend to be worrying about the internal dynamics between a yarn shop and its vendors.

"If she's around this weekend, I'll seek her out. If not, I'll email her when I get home," Hazel said.

Jenika said nothing more on the subject and led Hazel to the door, offering a polite smile that didn't quite reach her eyes. "You should have the schedule for tomorrow's events," she confirmed as they walked together.

"Yes, I have everything set for tomorrow. Thank you for checking," Hazel replied, a little disappointed that Shanice or Jules weren't the ones to end the evening's event and see her off.

"Well, goodnight then," Jenika said, almost rushing her out the door. "And thanks again, Hazel. We're so grateful you came."

Hazel paused and glanced one last time toward the now-quiet back room. "Please tell Shanice 'Thank you' for me. I'll see you both tomorrow," she said, raising her hand in farewell before stepping into the crisp night air.

In the car, as Marcus drove toward the hotel, Hazel gazed out the window, replaying the night in her mind. She thought about Melinda and Wren, the eager questions, and the connections she'd felt. However, the tense words she'd overheard coming from the back room were unsettling. The success of the evening, bright as it was, now felt just a little fragile, tainted by a gnawing sense of apprehension she couldn't quite identify.

"Did everything go okay tonight?" Marcus asked, catching her eye in the rearview mirror.

Hazel forced a small smile. "Yes...mostly." The hum of the car beneath her was soothing, though the lingering sense of disquiet remained. Whatever was happening back there, she reminded herself, it was none of my business. Her career was still delicate and too precious to risk over curiosity.

"Thank you for driving me around," she added, deciding to let the moment pass. "I won't need you again until my flight back home."

"Of course," Marcus replied. "I'll confirm everything twenty-four hours before your flight."

She murmured a quiet "Thanks," bringing the conversation to an end.

Hazel watched the town lights blur by, trying to convince herself to leave the tension of the evening behind and focus on the positives. As they approached the hotel, she couldn't shake the feeling that tonight's events would follow her longer than she wanted. Why hadn't they introduced her to Verna Shales, knowing her interest in collaborating? Why had Verna looked so displeased while examining the yarns? Was the yarn damaged?

Hazel's mind itched to uncover what was going on and to understand that unpleasant conversation in the back room. But she had to play it safe; there was too much at stake for her to lose. Yet, the persistent feeling that something was wrong wouldn't let go.

Chapter 8: Friday Morning

Hazel stepped out of her one-bedroom hotel room and onto the quiet, carpeted hallway, her pulse still a bit unsteady from the book signing the night before. She glanced back into the room, leaving stacks of workbooks organized on the dining table for the next day as the door clicked shut behind her. The evening had been a balm after a hectic year. Echoes of laughter, the clink of wine glasses, and warm conversations with Melinda and Wren, lingered in her mind. However, a few fragmented and unsettling words from a stranger at the end of the night in the back room left a tension at the base of her skull she couldn't quite shake.

Dressed in an oversized pullover from her book collection, the soft, heathered knit draped effortlessly over her frame. She styled it with a wide belt that cinched the sweater at her waist, emphasizing her shape and showcasing her silhouette. This balanced the cozy bulk of the pullover with a touch of refinement. Dark leggings hugged her curves and tucked neatly into worn, ankle-high leather boots that were both practical and stylish. Around her neck, she wore her ever-present scarf, a soft, patterned piece that had become her signature, adding a pop of color and warmth to her outfit. Together, these elements combined comfort with casual elegance, creating a perfect look for a day of teaching and connection.

She had been up early, preparing for day one of classes with a sense of eager purpose. Before heading to breakfast, she carefully arranged the classroom, placing workbooks at each seat and laying out swatches and samples. She wanted everything to be perfect, driven by a subtle but persistent worry that anything less might undermine her students' experience and her own belief that she deserved to be there.

The elevator ride down to the conference area, where she would be teaching all weekend, was short. As she descended to the ground floor, her phone chimed with a notification. Curious, she checked it and saw a comment on her social media post from the book signing: Melinda had written, "Thank you, Hazel! For the first time since my accident, I feel like I can make sweaters for the body I'm in. Ones that I'll actually love and feel comfortable wearing. Can't wait to get started today. I know class with Hazel is going to be epic!"

Hazel's face softened, and the last remnants of the previous night's tension melted away. This was why she did what she did—why she wrote *Sweaters That Fit*, why she taught, and why she encouraged others to trust their craft and their bodies.

The elevator doors slid open, and Hazel stepped into the bustling lobby. She navigated her way through the crowd of crocheters and knitters gathered for the retreat, exchanging nods and smiles with familiar faces from the previous evening's book signing event as she made her way to the large conference room designated for her classes. In addition to her sessions, three other designers were offering classes on topics ranging from spinning wool into yarn to techniques for giving amigurumi character personality to exploring various shawl constructions.

As Hazel stepped into her classroom, she surveyed the setup with satisfaction, double and triple checking every detail. Everything was just as she had left it an hour earlier: workbooks neatly placed at each table, yarn swatches in a rainbow of textures and hues spread out, and samples of finished projects arranged on a side table for inspiration.

Standing at the entrance, Hazel greeted each student as they began to trickle in, offering warm smiles while awkwardly exchanging small talk. To hide her trembling hands, she clasped them tightly behind her back. She took in the excitement and anticipation on each student's faces. The energy in the room grew, becoming infectious, and soon a cheerful hum filled the space.

Hazel glanced at her phone to check the time again—it was 9:45 a.m. Only fifteen minutes remained until the start of class. She scanned the room, hoping to spot Shanice. No sign of Shanice yet, Hazel thought, her fingers nervously drifting to her scarf. According to the schedule, Shanice was supposed to be here to introduce her before the class began. But she was nowhere in sight.

At the back of the room, Jenika sat hunched over her phone, an unmistakable frown creasing her brow. Concerned, Hazel crossed the room toward her. Jenika wore a crochet vest over a long-sleeve black tee with a deep V that revealed a tattoo on her clavicle reading "XI XI," flanked by flowing flowers. Her skirt billowed around her as she shifted in her seat, clearly tense.

"Jenika, is Shanice on her way?" Hazel asked gently, lowering her voice. "It's almost time to start."

Jenika barely looked up, shaking her head. "She was supposed to be here by now," she muttered, glancing back at her screen. "She's not answering any of my messages. I've checked with the other staff, and they haven't heard from her. Jules is busy assisting with the other teachers. She says she has no idea where Shanice is."

Hazel glanced around the room, feeling anxious to get started. The class buzzed with anticipation. Students seated and ready, some flipping through the workbook at their tables, while others were showing off the swatches they made for homework to their neighbors.

"What about her daughter? Does she know where her mom might be?" Hazel asked.

"No, she doesn't know. She's been out with a study group and hasn't been in touch with her mom," Jenika said, an unreadable look crossed her face that she quickly masked.

Hazel paused, uncertain about what to do next. "Do you want me to wait a little while longer or start on time?" she asked, pulling up the schedule on her phone. She had memorized it but wanted to double-check that it was accurate before speaking. "The plan was for Shanice to kick things off here this morning and introduce me," she said, her voice wavering slightly as she reread the email.

She swallowed the lump forming in her throat, feeling a bead of sweat gather at the back of her neck. Okay, Whitely, girl. This isn't what was planned, but we will figure it out like we always do. Come on, you can do this, she thought, tamping down her growing anxiety. With a final mental shake, she steadied herself, resigned to do the unexpected.

Jenika sighed and slipped her phone back into her pocket, glancing at the group of students filling the seats. "No, go ahead. She'd want us to stick to the schedule," she said, looking toward the door and bouncing her knees nervously under her long skirt.

Brushing off the discomfort settling over her, Hazel nodded. At precisely 10 a.m. she moved to the front of the room and called everyone to attention with a welcoming smile and an overview of the day. "Today, we're diving into the essentials—swatching, gauge, and learning how to make a garment that fits your body," she said, her voice warm and confident. The room hummed with focus and collective determination as Hazel launched into the content. The first few hours flew by, and when she was ready to announce a sixty-minute lunch break, she glanced around, still seeing no sign of Shanice.

"Alright, great job, everyone." Hazel praised. It wasn't an easy session for many students, but they persevered and grasped the material. She felt proud of their efforts. "Let's take a break for lunch. Use that time to relax and clear your heads. We covered a lot so far. As you take this time, reflect on what we've learned. Don't get overwhelmed or discouraged. When we come back together, we'll practice a few exercises from the workbook to reinforce our understanding."

The room released a collective sigh as the students began to disperse. She scanned the room again, still no Shanice.

Hazel sent Jenika a questioning glance. Jenika shrugged and approached Hazel at the front of the class, her lips pressed into a tight line. "Shanice is still not responding to any of my messages. I need to check on her," she said, her voice tinged with worry. "Would you come with me?" she asked, her face full of concern.

Hazel hesitated, contemplating the timing. The break was only for sixty minutes, and she didn't want to disrupt her class schedule or get mixed up in something that didn't concern her. "I don't know. Can't Jules go?" she said, tugging at her scarf and glancing back at the students still mingling about. What would Whitley do? she thought.

"Jules is busy handling all the other teachers. She's needed here. I'm really worried about Shanice," Jenika said, sensing Hazel's reluctance beginning to crack. "The shop is only a short drive. We'll be there and back in plenty of time to resume class," she reassured, her tone imploring.

"Oh, okay. Of course, I'll go with you. But let's go straight there and back. No detours, okay?"

Hazel's concern deepened as they walked through the automatic doors together. As they crossed the hotel parking lot, Hazel followed, unsure what type of car Jenika drove. Her steps faltered when Jenika pulled out a key fob and unlocked a brand-new red Mustang convertible with leather seats. Not exactly what she had expected from a full-time yarn store employee and part-time student. Jenika pressed the start button, and the car purred to life as they left the hotel parking lot.

They made the quick drive to the shop. Jenika parked on the yellow lines directly in front of the store. Sensing Hazel's concern at the 'NO PARKING' sign directly in front, Jenika reassured her, "We'll be really quick," before exiting the car.

Outside the shop, a sign posted on the door announced it would be closed for the morning due to the retreat. However, as they approached, something felt off. Jenika pulled out a separate keyring to open the door, but Hazel's hand shot out to grip her arm.

"Jenika," she whispered.

"What?" Jenika asked, glancing over her shoulder, confused.

"Look! The door. It's open."

Jenika's eyes widened as she noticed the gap in the door. "It shouldn't be. The store isn't supposed to be open," she explained. "What should we do? Should we call the police?" Jenika asked, her voice taut with fear.

Hazel hesitated for a moment, her mind racing trying to find a rational explanation. There was no reason for the doors to be unlocked. Perhaps Shanice had come in to catch up on work and lost track of time, distracted and unaware that the door hadn't closed behind her. "Let's check to make sure everything is okay before we get the police involved," she suggested.

Hazel gently pushed the door, and it swung wide without resistance, revealing a quiet and shadowy shop. "Stay behind me," she whispered to Jenika, uncertain if they were making the right decision by not calling the authorities.

The usual warm and welcoming atmosphere that greeted customers was absent. Shelves lined with colorful skeins of yarn cast long, somber shadows in the autumn light pouring through the bay windows, the vibrant colors muted in the stillness. A faint chill lingered in the air, prickling Hazel's skin.

"Shanice?" Hazel called, her voice sounding unnaturally loud in the silence. They waited and listened, but there was no answer. They exchanged uneasy glances and crept farther inside the shop, instinctively moving toward the back room where Shanice often worked.

Tension buzzed in the air as they silently navigated around tables piled high with yarn and notions, careful not to make any noise.

"It doesn't appear to be a break-in. The cash register area seems undisturbed, and the shop appears as it always does," Jenika whispered, a half-step behind Hazel.

Hazel didn't respond; tension coiled inside her. As they neared the back room, the hairs on the back of her neck stood on ends with anticipation.

"Shanice, are you here?" Hazel's voice trembled slightly as they reached the door.

The door stood ajar, and the room was dark.

"Shanice, it's Jenika and Hazel. Are you in there?"

Hazel placed her hand on the doorknob and paused. She looked over her shoulder at Jenika, who nodded and mouthed, "Do it". Taking a deep breath, Hazel pushed the door open.

Light from the store's bay windows streamed in, and Hazel's stomach dropped as bile rose in her throat. She struggled to move; her legs felt like cement. Jenika gasped behind her.

The sight before them was something Hazel would never be able to forget. They had found her.

There, slumped over skeins of yarn, Shanice sat at her desk, her head turned toward the door. Her eyes were wide open, staring blankly, her skin pale and lifeless. Hazel's breath caught when she saw the striking blue glass drop spindle with yellow and white swirls protruding from Shanice's neck, a surreal and horrifying contrast against her ashen skin.

Is that the spindle I held last night? Hazel thought.

Before she could think any further, Hazel rushed to Shanice's side, desperate to find a sign of life. Maybe there's still time. Maybe there's something we can do, she thought, pressing her fingers to Shanice's inner wrist, like she had seen done on TV.

"Oh...oh my God..." Jenika's voice came out in a strangled whisper, her face drained of color. "Is she de-" she screeched, unable to finish the word.

Hazel felt herself teeter; the world swaying as the reality of what had happened sank in. "I can't feel a pulse," she whispered, glancing over at Jenika, who looked ready to faint.

Shaking off her own shock, Hazel rushed to the younger woman's side. There was nothing she could do for Shanice now, but she could help Jenika.

Hazel reached out and gripped Jenika's arm to steady them both. She turned Jenika to face her, forcing her to look away from Shanice's lifeless face. "Jenika," she said, her voice calm and urgent, cutting through the shock. "Shanice is dead. Someone did this to her. We have to call the police. Now."

Chapter 9: Friday Afternoon

Outside, the flashing lights of patrol cars and an ambulance cast eerie shadows over the walls lined with yarn and cluttered tabletops. The shop, usually a haven of creativity, felt suffocating under the weight of tragedy. Teams of people dusted surfaces for fingerprints and took photos, creating a mess in the process.

Hazel sat next to Jenika in the shop's cozy nook, both wrapped in blankets hastily provided by the paramedics. Hazel glanced around the shop filled with police officers and forensic teams, but there were no crocheters or knitters in sight. Dead bodies aren't good for business, she thought ruefully.

Jenika trembled, visibly shaken, her hands clutching the edges of her blanket as if it were the only thing tethering her to reality. Hazel couldn't begin to imagine what the younger woman was going through after finding her boss brutally murdered. Though equally disturbed, Hazel forced herself to stay composed. She couldn't afford to let her emotions surface, not now, not in front of strangers. Instead, she focused on the hum of activity around her, whispered voices, heavy footsteps, and the occasional crackle of a police radio.

The spell broke when two coroners emerged from the back room, dressed in dark clothes adorned with 'CORONER' in white lettering across their jackets. They pushed a gurney with a black bag. Hazel's stomach twisted at the sight. The unmistakable shape of the bag left no room for doubt: it contained a dead body...Shanice's dead body.

Hazel tracked the gurney all the way through the front door and out of sight, releasing a breath she hadn't realized she was holding. She glanced back at the office, wishing this was all a bad dream she could wake up from. But it wasn't a dream. This was real.

An older woman dressed in blue coveralls walked out of the office, exuding an air of authority. She removed her oversized protective eyeglasses and pushed back the hood of her suit, revealing a vibrant blue-and-yellow Ankara cap snugly covering her hair.

With a clipboard in hand, she strode purposefully toward the detective in charge. Detective Ridley stood in the middle of the room with his arms crossed over an aged, rumpled trench coat as he surveyed the scene. When he first arrived, Hazel was shocked. She had never been in a situation like this before, having to interact with police. Detective Ridley was nothing like she'd expected; a coffee stain on his shirt that looked old and fraying edges of his coat betrayed his authority.

He glanced at the woman and then back to writing in his notebook. "What do you have for me, Doc?" he asked, his voice gruff but expectant.

"Nothing conclusive yet," she replied, her tone measured and detached. "Initial findings suggest she died between 9:30 and 10:30 last night. However," she added, tilting her head slightly, her words drifting over to the nook, "we can't determine the exact cause of death yet. There is not enough blood at the scene, which suggests that the puncture wound from the spindle in her neck was not the fatal blow. She was stabbed post-mortem. I'll have more answers once we get her back to the lab and conduct an autopsy."

Detective Ridley nodded as he continued to make notes, his jaw tightening. "Anything else I should know for now?"

"There are fingerprints on the spindle," she said, tapping her clipboard lightly. "But that's to be expected; it's a tool in the shop that many people have handled. We'll process them and send over the results," she stated matter-of-factly. Without waiting for further questions, she turned and walked out of the shop with brisk efficiency.

Jenika whimpered, doubling over with her head in her hands. Hazel remained silent, her dry throat too tight to form words. She carefully placed a comforting hand on Jenika's back, trying hard to avoid any ink residue from her fingerprinting getting on her crochet vest.

"How strange," Hazel thought, noticing the juxtaposition between the shop's vibrancy, with its colorful yarns, samples, and notions, and the bland and colorless hues of the police and forensic teams. This place, which represented joy and creativity, had become a place of sadness. Hazel reflected on her first experience at a yarn shop and how its magic completely changed her life. Looking around, she saw the magic had dimmed here.

Detective Ridley walked over, standing a few feet away with the little notebook in hand. His expression was a mix of irritation and exhaustion, a man worn down by nearly three decades on the job. Stocky and tall, with a balding head and watery eyes that conveyed an air of perpetual cynicism, he exuded the weary detachment of someone counting down the days to retirement. His faded blue shirt and tomato sauce-stained tie didn't inspire much confidence. Under his gaze, Hazel felt a prickle of unease.

"Let's go through it again from the top; how you came to know the celebrated musical sensation, Shanice Keller, and what you're doing here," he said in a gruff tone.

For the second time, Hazel recounted the events leading to Shanice's discovery, struggling to keep her voice steady. She had already told the story to the young patrol officer who first arrived at the scene, but now Detective Ridley made her relive it all over again.

Hazel swallowed hard, her brows furrowed as she recalled the night before, "I finished my book signing, mingled a bit, and spoke to a few people afterwards. Everyone left."

"And what time was that?" Detective Ridley asked.

"It was around 8:45 p.m. when Jenika walked me out. I don't know who else was still here at the shop after the last customers left. The staff was cleaning up while I packed my bags. Once I was ready, I went looking for Shanice to say goodnight and thank her for the event. I could hear Shanice talking to someone in her office, but I didn't know who it was. Just before I reached the office, Jenika appeared to walk me out," Hazel explained.

"Did you see anyone besides Jenika?" Detective Ridley continued.

"The only person I saw was Jenika. She mentioned that Shanice and Jules were around, but I didn't actually see them."

Detective Ridley made notes in his notebook. "Okay, walk me through what led to your visit to the shop today," he instructed, still not looking at her, his voice flat and emotionless. "And you're sure you didn't notice anything unusual before finding the body?" Detective Ridley pressed, maintaining his monotonous tone.

"No, Detective," Hazel replied firmly, keeping her voice steady. "As I mentioned before, Shanice was supposed to be at the hotel to introduce me before the start of my class—it was on the retreat schedule. When she didn't show up and didn't respond to any of Jenika's messages, we came to the shop to look for her. That's when we found her."

Detective Ridley sighed, rubbed the bridge of his nose, and tilted his face toward the ceiling with eyes closed. "Just my luck. Less than thirty days from retirement, and I've got a murder on my hands."

Hazel resisted the urge to roll her eyes; this wasn't about him. She angrily rubbed at a bit of ink still on her right thumb where they'd taken her elimination prints. She felt bile rise in her throat at the thought that she had touched the spindle that killed Shanice. Not only that, but the evening before, she had taken photos of it and posted it on her social media, admiring its beauty. Now, it lay in a plastic evidence bag, covered in blood. It wasn't very pretty anymore.

Jenika sniffled quietly beside her. Detective Ridley glanced at her briefly but said nothing, turning back to Hazel. "That's all for now, Ms. Whitmore. You can return to your hotel."

Hazel hesitated, remembering. "Jenika drove me here. I don't have a ride back," she said.

Detective Ridley waved dismissively at the uniformed officer stationed near the front door. "Brooks," he called.

Officer Brooks rushed over to them. "Sir," he said.

Detective Ridley continued scribbling in his notebook without looking up. "Give Ms. Whitmore a ride back to her hotel," he ordered.

Office Brooks didn't look too thrilled about playing driver. "Yes, Sir."

Detective Ridley turned to Hazel and said sternly, "Ms. Whitmore, don't leave town. We'll need you to come down to the station for a formal interview." With that, she was dismissed.

Hazel stood, reluctant to leave Jenika behind. "Are you going to be okay?" she asked softly.

Jenika raised her head, her tear-streaked face surprisingly composed and her voice steady. "I'll be fine. I've called Jules to let her know what's happened."

"Find me at the hotel if you need anything," Hazel offered gently.

Jenika nodded.

Hazel followed Officer Brooks out to his squad car, the chilly air biting at her skin still warm from the interview. She slid into the back seat, the door closing with a heavy thud. The short drive to the hotel stretched ahead of her, even as her mind raced far faster than the car could ever go.

Shanice's words from the night before drifted back to her: "Get ready for a night to remember." Hazel let out a hollow laugh under her breath, leaning her head against the cool glass of the window.

Memorable, indeed, she thought. But not in the way anyone ever expected.

Chapter 10: Friday Afternoon

The squad car rolled to a stop in front of the hotel, its engine rumbling like a distant thunder. Officer Brooks stepped out and opened the back door. Hazel climbed out, feeling the weight of his eyes on her as she walked toward the automatic doors. Her pulse quickened, and a flicker of paranoia rippled through her. Was he still watching her? She glanced over her shoulder, but Officer Brooks was already back in the driver's seat.

The lobby greeted her with the familiar hum of retreat energy: groups of crocheters and knitters chatting, their voices melding into a low buzz. But Hazel couldn't shake the feeling that the room shifted when she walked in, the weight of curious glances pressing down on her.

How did I end up in this position? she thought, her stomach twisted with regret. I should have refused to go with Jenika when she asked.

As she crossed the lobby, her steps faltered. There they were, Jules and Selene, heads bowed together in quiet conspiracy, their faces drawn close as they whispered. Hazel couldn't hear them, but the sight sent a chill crawling up her spine.

Jules glanced up first, catching sight of her, and nudged Selene. Both women straightened as their gazes locked with Hazel's. For a moment, no one moved, the space between them heavy with unspoken words. Then, without so much as a nod, they split. Jules strode purposefully into one of the classrooms, and Selene made her way toward the elevators, her back stiff and unyielding.

Hazel's throat tightened, but she forced herself to keep walking. Whatever was happening, she couldn't let it derail her now. She had students depending on her. Outside her classroom, she paused, her fingers grazing the handle. She closed her eyes and drew in a slow, deliberate breath, trying to steady the storm inside her chest.

The image of Shanice's lifeless body flashed behind her closed eyelids; those vacant gray eyes seared into her memories. Her breath hitched, but she gritted her teeth and shook it off. Not now. You can fall apart later. Her students waited, and Whitley, the version of herself she leaned on in moments of crisis, needed to take the lead again.

When she finally opened the door, the classroom greeted her with an undercurrent of tension. Students clustered in small groups, calculators and workbooks spread out on tables as they whispered about sweater adjustments. Others sat crocheting and knitting, their hands moving in a steady rhythm, though their faces carried a shadow of the day's chaos.

"Hello, everyone," Hazel greeted, her voice steady but softer than usual. Heads turned toward her, and she felt their quiet anticipation.

She walked to the front of the room, every step an act of will. Still shaken, she took one more deep breath and launched into the lesson, her words clear and focused. The day's events lingered at the edges of her mind, but Hazel pushed through, determined not to let her students down. Whatever storm awaited outside this room, it would have to wait.

"Apologies for the delay in resuming after lunch," Hazel began, her voice steady but tight. "There was an...incident." The words hung in the air like a weight. Hazel forced herself not to flinch under the expectant gazes of her students. She hated being late or off schedule, but this wasn't her fault. Still, the lingering embarrassment gnawed at her. "Any questions about where we left off?" she continued briskly, her tone calm and professional.

She hoped to steer the conversation back to the workbooks and out of the landmine of rumors. The news about Shanice's death had undoubtedly spread through the retreat by now, but she wasn't about to fan the flames.

For a brief moment, the room was silent. Then, a hand went up tentatively. Her name tag read Cynthia.

"Yes, Cynthia?" Hazel prompted, hesitantly.

The woman, dressed in a colorful freeform crochet beret that matched her purple hair, stood. Her eyes darted nervously around the room, as if seeking permission to speak. Finally, she cleared her throat. "I know I'm not the only one wondering what happened at the shop."

A wave of murmurs swept through the room. Hazel's chest tightened as all eyes locked onto her. Her heart pounded, but she forced herself to channel Whitley, the composed, no-nonsense version of herself who didn't flinch under pressure.

"I'm not allowed to discuss the details of the investigation," Hazel said carefully. "It's an active investigation, and Detective Ridley will be addressing everyone later this evening to answer questions. That's all I can say for now," she said firmly, her tone measured.

Her words left no room for argument, but the air bristled with worry and fear.

"Are we safe here?" a woman asked.

Another voice joined in, sharper this time, "Should we be worried?"

Hazel raised her hand in her calming gesture. "The detective has reassured us that there's no immediate danger. He will explain every detail tonight. Until then, please let's focus on the material we're here to learn." Hazel's voice was firm, leaving no room for further discussion on the topic, though her palms felt clammy against the desk. "If there are no other questions about the material, let's move on."

The room buzzed with whispers, but slowly, reluctantly, the energy shifted back to the lesson. Hazel pressed forward, guiding the class through adjustments, stitch calculations, and pattern modifications. Her focus remained sharp, even as an undercurrent of tension lingering in the air.

By the time the session wrapped up, the atmosphere was subdued but cooperative. Hazel let out a quiet sigh of relief as the last student filed out of the room. She had made it through the first day, but the weight of the day's events clung to her like a shadow.

Chapter 11: Friday Evening

The door clicked shut, leaving the classroom empty and Hazel in silence. She methodically moved around the room, collecting abandoned scraps of paper from the tables and stray swatches, her fingers brushing against the soft wool and cotton. The buzz she'd felt earlier evaporated. The rush of standing in front of a room full of crocheters and knitters, guiding them through the nuances of swatching, sweater math, and pattern adjustments so their finished sweaters would fit, had drained away like a receding tide.

Her steps slowed as the weight of the day settled on her shoulders, heavier than the pile of materials she was carrying. Hazel set them down on the table at the front of the room and lowered herself onto a nearby chair, her knees buckling as if they had been holding her up all day.

She sank deep into the seat, her breath escaping in a shaky sigh. The fluorescent lights above buzzed softly, casting stark shadows across the room. For a moment, she stared at the swatch in her hand, a simple rectangle of stockinette stitch, uneven but earnest. She allowed herself to feel the magnitude of it all, the events of earlier hitting her hard.

Her mind replayed the murmur of concerned voices, the pointed questions, and unspoken fears simmering beneath the surface. *Are we safe?* The question still clung to her, pressing against her chest.

Shanice's lifeless face flashed in her mind, sending a shiver through her. She felt dizzy and lightheaded; her breathing became fast and ragged.

Hazel placed her head between her knees and took slow, deliberate breaths.

"Here, drink this," came a familiar voice. Hazel recognized the tattooed hand that appeared, holding a bottle of water under her nose. It was Jenika.

She took the bottle, twisted off the cap, and tipped her head back, drinking hungrily.

It took Hazel a few moments to regain control of her breathing enough to speak. "Thank you," she whispered, her voice raspy.

"Are you okay?" Jenika asked, concern etched across her face.

"Yeah, I'm okay," Hazel replied, offering a small reassuring smile. She took a cleansing breath and remembered to ask Jenika what had happened at the shop with Detective Ridley after she left. "How was your interview with Detective Ridley?"

Jenika's expression changed, her eyes becoming unreadable. Hazel's thoughts drifted from a million possible scenarios. "Was it that bad? Are you okay?" she asked.

As if recognizing that her face was giving too much away, Jenika plastered a forced smile on her lips. "No, it was fine. He just wanted to fill in some gaps."

"Such as...?" Hazel prompted.

Jenika shrugged and moved to the next table, collecting material left behind by the students. In a low voice, she said, "He mainly asked about what time I left the shop last night and who else was there."

"And?" Hazel pressed.

"I told him Jules was there too, but I don't know if that was everyone. I didn't notice anything out of the ordinary. I just left."

Jenika turned her back on Hazel as she walked to the next table. After a long moment, she said, "I wish I'd paid more attention."

"You didn't know," Hazel reassured. "Maybe if you had stayed, you would have been in danger too."

Jenika turned back to face Hazel, her eyes filled with tears. "Yes, I suppose you're right," she said, wiping a stray tear from her cheek and forcing a smile.

Hazel looked at the younger woman, sensing something was off. A guarded look crossed Jenika's face. Hazel wasn't sure what it was, but she was convinced Jenika was holding something back. Whatever it was, Hazel couldn't tell.

With shaky legs, Hazel stood up slowly. "I'll finish up here," she said with a sigh, glancing around the classroom. "You should go have dinner. Detective Ridley will be here to meet with us all soon."

"Yes, and you too. When was the last time you ate anything? Get some food in your stomach," Jenika replied before exiting the classroom.

Hazel remained, staring after Jenika and feeling that something wasn't right. Did she witness something the night Shanice was murdered and was too scared to speak about it?

What now? Hazel thought, staring at the closed classroom door. She knew she couldn't stay here forever, but the thought of stepping back into the retreat's evening events, where whispers and sideways glances awaited her, made her stomach churn.

Hazel was tired.

She allowed herself a moment to gather the strength she would need to face whatever came next.

Chapter 12: Later Friday Evening

Later that evening, the classroom was packed wall-to-wall with retreat attendees and teachers, the air thick with uncertainty. Whispers swirled through the room like threads of unfinished projects, frayed and tense. Hazel stood near the back, trying hard to blend into the crowd, though she could feel curious glances and quiet speculations settling on her.

At the front of the room, Detective Ridley loomed. He wore the same clothes as earlier and looked more disheveled than before. Hazel hoped his detective skills were better than his fashion sense. His expression was unreadable, and his voice cutting through the murmurs with his signature curtness.

"We're still in the early stages of the investigation," he began, his flat and deliberate. "This remains an active case, and we're exploring every possibility. I'll need full cooperation from everyone. That means staying available for further questioning and not leaving town without notifying us."

His words hung heavy in the room.

Selene Hopkins raised her hand and stood without waiting to be called on, with the kind of theatrical flair that suggested she was addressing an adoring crowd rather than a room full of wary faces.

"Detective Ridley," she began, her voice smooth and confident, "I believe I could be of some assistance." She placed a delicate hand over her chest. "As someone with a considerable following and influence in this community, people naturally look to me for guidance. Perhaps I could serve as a sort of liaison between you and the attendees?" she said, her tone tinged with incredulity.

The room stilled, and the hum of whispered conversations was replaced by an almost collective eye roll. Hazel felt her lips twitch in an involuntary smirk. Of course, Selene would find a way to center herself in all of this.

Detective Ridley raised his eyebrows and blinked at her, impassive but faintly amused. "A liaison?" he repeated, his blunt voice tinged with dry skepticism.

Selene's smile didn't falter. "Yes, someone who can keep the group informed, maintain morale, and—"

"Maintain morale?" Detective Ridley cut in, his tone sharp enough to cut yarn. "This isn't a team-building retreat, Ms. Hopkins. It's a murder investigation."

The room rippled with a mix of gasps and muffled chuckles. Selene's smile froze, the slightest crack showing in her polished veneer. She shifted on her feet and cleared her throat. "I only meant that—"

Detective Ridley didn't let her finish. "Right. I appreciate the offer, but I don't need a spokesperson. I need cooperation. Let's keep the focus on that."

The air seemed to shift. A few attendees exchanged amused glances, quickly schooling their faces back to neutrality. Selene sank back into her seat, her cheeks flushed.

Detective Ridley's gaze swept over the room, settling briefly on Hazel before moving on. "The best way you can assist us is by answering questions when asked and staying out of the way. We don't want anyone getting in the way or, worse, getting hurt." He paused, his eyes narrowing slightly. "If anyone has information, anything at all, even if it doesn't seem relevant, no matter how small, speak to me or one of my officers. And don't spread rumors or speculate. That's not going to help anyone."

A voice from the back of the room interrupted, sharp and shaky. "Was it a robbery gone wrong? Are we even safe here?" they asked, obviously scared.

The question hung in the air for a moment before the room broke into a cacophony of voices.

"What about security? Shouldn't the hotel be doing more?"

"Are they going to lock down the retreat?"

"Why haven't we been told more about what happened?"

The murmurs grew louder, overlapping like tangled threads, some laced with fear and others with frustration. Hazel felt the tension rising, the distress rippling through the crowd like an electric current.

Detective Ridley shook his head and raised a hand to calm the growing agitation. His expression softened slightly as he spoke. "We have no reason to believe there's an ongoing threat. We're exploring every possibility. I understand you're all concerned, but speculations will only make things worse. But stay alert and report anything unusual."

The murmurs subsided, though a low hum of anxiety lingered. Detective Ridley's jaw tightened as he scanned the room with a steady and authoritative gaze. "Let me be clear. This was not a random act. It was not a robbery gone wrong. At this time, we have no reason to believe there is an ongoing threat to anyone here."

Hazel didn't miss the way he phrased it—"at this time". The reassurance felt paper-thin, and judging by the uneasy glances exchanged around the room, the attendees weren't entirely convinced either.

"But how can we be sure?" another voice piped up, this time from a man near the front. A double pointed knitting needle clutched tightly in his hands, his project abandoned in his lap. "People don't just die like this without warning."

Detective Ridley's expression visibly hardened. "That's what we're working to find out. The best way you can help is by remaining calm, staying put, and letting us do our job."

The room quieted, though tension still crackled in the air. He opened the floor for more questions, hoping to quell the group's worry. After a few more exchanges, he closed out questions. "Try to enjoy the rest of your retreat. We are doing everything we can to get this resolved," he reassured, his tone surprisingly gentle.

He dismissed the attendees, requesting only the Yarn-monious staff remain behind for individual interviews.

As the room began to empty, the soft hum of retreat attendees' murmurs faded into the background. Hazel remained standing in the back, her gaze fixed on Detective Ridley. His sharp eyes scanned the room, lingering on each retreat staff member for just a beat too long, as if weighing their presence against some unspoken measure.

A chill prickled at the back of Hazel's neck. She felt uneasy again. She rubbed her temples, exhaustion pressing down on her. The day's events played on a loop in her mind, tangled like yarn gone awry.

"Ms. Whitmore," Detective Ridley called out as he approached her, his heavy footsteps breaking the silence. "If you think of anything, anything at all, that you didn't mention earlier, you'll let me know, won't you?"

Hazel met his gaze, forcing herself to hold it steady. "Of course, Detective," she replied, her voice even, though her pulse quickened.

He nodded once, his expression unreadable, then dismissed her.

As the last retreat attendees filed out, Hazel lingered behind, staring at the near-empty classroom. The Yarn-monious staff clustered together, with Jules and Detective Ridley at the center, speaking with a uniform officer, the same one who drove her back to the hotel. The vibrant energy that had filled the space earlier—the chatter of students comparing stitches and the occasional triumphant exclamation over a perfectly executed modification—was gone, replaced by a heavy silence. Hazel let out a shaky breath.

Unable to face anyone else, she decided to retreat to her room instead of going to dinner in the dining room set up for the retreat. The walk down the hotel hallway felt longer than usual, the muted beige walls closing in on her with each step.

Once inside her room, she locked the door and leaned against it, allowing her bag to slip from her shoulder to the floor. She exhaled deeply, her body sagging with the weight of the day. Everything about the murder scene nagged at her. There was something strange about it; something that didn't sit right.

She replayed the events in her mind, searching for the elusive thread that felt out of place. Shanice's body, the glass drop spindle, the shelves of yarn undisturbed, the retreat schedule. Hazel couldn't pinpoint it, but the feeling gnawed at her like an unfinished puzzle missing its final piece.

The muffled sounds of laughter and conversation drifted through the walls from the hallway. Hazel rubbed her arms, trying to shake the growing fear and disquiet.

"I just need to survive this weekend, and then I can go home," she muttered to herself.

She certainly didn't want to get involved in something so grim, but her instincts told her there was more to Shanice's death than met the eye. Though she wanted to ignore it, it wasn't in her nature to shy away from situations that didn't involve her if she could help.

For now, though, Hazel kicked off her shoes and sank onto the edge of the couch. She needed rest, and clarity. Tomorrow would bring new light, and perhaps, a clearer picture of what felt so wrong.

Chapter 13: Early Saturday Morning

The shrill ring of Hazel's phone shattered the predawn stillness, jerking her awake. Who could be calling so early. Disoriented, she squinted at the screen. St. Louis Missouri Police Department. Her stomach twisted as she tapped to answer.

"Hello?" she rasped, her voice thick with sleep.

"This is Detective Ridley from the STMPD," came the gruff voice. "I need you to answer a few more questions about Shanice Keller's murder. Meet me in the dining room of your hotel in thirty minutes."

Before Hazel could respond, the line went dead.

Well, I'm awake now. Hazel swung her legs over the edge of the bed, her heart pounding as she tried to shake off the lingering fog of sleep. What else could he possibly want? The tension tightened in her chest as she hurried to get ready.

She showered quickly, then applied her makeup with practiced efficiency, her hands steady despite the storm brewing within her. From the dresser, she selected a sapphire blue cardigan adorned with an intricate cable and lace pattern—one of her designs from the book—and layered it over a simple black pant jumpsuit. Knee-high black boots completed the ensemble, grounding her with their familiar weight. After carefully untying the silk scarf from her head, she caught a fleeting glance at herself in the full-length mirror by the door. Her reflection looked composed. She tied on her scarf and slipped quietly out of the room.

Twenty-five minutes later, Hazel sat at a secluded table in the corner of the dining room. The space was empty except for her and a few staff members bustling to set up the breakfast buffet. She cradled a glass of cranberry juice, her untouched made-to-order spinach and mushroom omelet growing cold on the plate before her, her appetite dulled by the nervousness swirling in her stomach.

Detective Ridley strode in, his expression as menacing as his wrinkled suit. Without so much as a greeting, he sank into the chair across from her, his intense gaze locking onto hers like a hawk sizing up its prey.

"Is there anything from the night of your book signing that you need to tell me?" he began, his tone loaded with suspicion.

Hazel straightened, unnerved by the implication. "I told you everything I can think of," she said carefully, her tone carrying a hint of defensiveness. She muttered under her breath, "Though clearly, you think otherwise."

She stabbed her fork into her omelet, taking a bite to cover the simmering frustration. The once fluffy eggs now felt laden on her tongue, the taste tainted by the bitterness of the conversation.

Detective Ridley's eyes narrowed, but he didn't respond to her remark. "Was there an argument at the shop that night?" he pressed, slowly annunciating each word.

Hazel hesitated, recalling the muffled voices she'd heard. "Well...yes," she admitted. "While I was packing up, I heard Shanice speaking loudly to someone."

Detective Ridley leaned forward, his pen poised over his small black notebook. "And you didn't think to mention that during your interview?" His tone carried an edge of disbelief, and he rubbed a hand over his face in frustration. "Who was she arguing with?"

Hazel's brow furrowed as she tried to piece the memory together. "I don't know," she admitted. "At first, I thought it was Jenika or Jules. I assumed it was just the four of us left in the shop after the attendees had gone." She paused, her voice faltering. "But then Jenika came to walk me out, and Shanice was still talking to someone. Maybe it was Jules, but I hadn't seen her since the book signing started, and I don't know if any of the other staff were there."

"Did you recognize the other voice?" he asked, his tone sharper. "Could you tell if it was a man or a woman?"

Hazel shook her head. "No, I didn't recognize the voice. It was hard to tell with the music playing, but I think it might have been a woman's voice."

Detective Ridley's expression darkened. "Why didn't you tell me all this yesterday?"

Hazel's irritation flared. "I didn't think of it until now. Everything happened so fast," she said defensively, then quickly softened her tone. "I'd never seen a murder before, so forgive me for not recalling everything exactly."

Detective Ridley's sharp gaze pinned her in place. "What exactly did you hear?" he asked, as if he didn't hear Hazel's explanation.

Hazel's mind churned, sifting through the fog of memory. She felt heat creeping up her neck. "I don't know," she admitted, her words flustered and uncertain. "Not much. Just fragments." She closed her eyes briefly, forcing herself to focus. "Something about a 'illegal scheme' and...'you'll pay.'"

Detective Ridley scribbled furiously in his notebook. "An illegal scheme? In a yarn shop?" His voice carried a note of skepticism, like an incredulous eyeroll.

He looked up at Hazel, his sharp eyes narrowing. "Is there anything else you're conveniently remembering now?"

Hazel's cheeks flushed with irritation. "No. That's all."

Without warning, Detective Ridley stood, his chair scraping loudly against the floor. The table jostled, and Hazel barely caught her juice before it spilled. He stared at her for a moment, his jaw tight, then turned and stalked out of the room without another word.

Hazel let out a shaky breath, her hands trembling as she pushed her now cold omelet aside.

"Just breathe," she whispered to herself, the words trembling on her lips. "You'll be home in a few days. You can get through this."

She reached for her scarf, wrapping it tight around her neck. The soft fabric, usually a source of comfort, now offered a fragile barrier against the icy dread spreading through her veins.

She remained seated long after Detective Ridley left, her thoughts spiraling. She should have brought her sock project, something, anything, to keep her hands busy. But in her rush to meet the detective, she hadn't been thinking. And now, she felt trapped, frozen in place, unable to summon the strength to move.

Why had she gone with Jenika to the shop? The question clawed at her. She should have refused more forcefully, should have trusted her instincts to mind her own business and stay out of anything that didn't affect her. But that wasn't who she was. Hazel could never ignore someone in visible distress, not when she knew she could help.

Look where that had gotten her.

Her chest tightened as the weight of the situation settled over her. She, Hazel Whitmore, who prided herself on living a quiet, unassuming life, had somehow become entangled in a murder investigation. She'd never even had a speeding ticket, and now, she's embroiled in something far darker and far messier than she could have imagined.

Panic began to rise, sharp and suffocating. Hazel closed her eyes, forcing herself to take slow, deliberate breaths. *In through the nose, out through the mouth. Steady.* Her heartbeat gradually slowed, the edges of her panic dulling enough for her thoughts to clear.

Think, she commanded herself. *What can you do?*

There was more to Shanice's murder. Hazel could feel it.

Chapter 14: Saturday Morning

Back in her room, Hazel couldn't go back to sleep. Her early morning conversation with Detective Ridley replayed in her mind, each detail picking at her nerves. She tried to distract herself by organizing the workbooks for her next class, lining them up neatly in rows, but the tension lingered, coiling tighter in her chest. The day hadn't even fully started, and she already had a splitting headache.

Eventually, she gave up. Exhausted but restless, Hazel found herself back in the dining room, surrendering to her desperate need for caffeine. She rarely drank coffee while traveling, but this morning called for it. At the coffee station, she poured a steaming cup, stirring in an excessive amount of creamer and sugar, her movements mechanical.

"Hazel! There you are!"

The sudden voice made her jump. Hazel turned to see Jenika rushing toward her, breathless, her face lit up with excitement.

"Did you hear the news?" Jenika asked, practically vibrating with energy.

Hazel frowned, her tired mind struggling to keep up. "What news?"

"They caught her!" Jenika said, lowering her voice but unable to suppress her giddy excitement.

"Wait, what?" Hazel blinked, her pulse quickening. "Caught who?"

"Shanice's killer!" Jenika practically squealed, bouncing on her toes like a child on Christmas morning. "It's over. They arrested her!"

Hazel's stomach churned. "Hold on," she said, her voice sharpening. "Start from the beginning. What are you talking about?"

Jenika glanced around the bustling dining room, retreat attendees chatting and loading up their plates. She grabbed Hazel's arm and tugged her toward a quiet corner table.

"Okay," Jenika began, leaning in close, her tone conspiratorial. "So, last night, after everyone left, that detective, Ridley, or whatever, interviewed all the staff. He was asking if anything strange had happened recently. That's when I remembered the argument during your book signing. You remember? There was shouting in the back room?"

Hazel frowned, trying to piece it together. "Sort of. I didn't hear much. What was going on?"

"Well," Jenika hesitated, glancing around again before dropping her voice to a whisper, "I hate airing people's dirty laundry, but Shanice was arguing with Verna."

"Verna?" Hazel's eyebrows shot up in surprise.

Jenika nodded. "Yes, Verna Shales. The dyer from Sunset Fiber Works; the one here for the trunk show this weekend at the shop."

Hazel's memory clicked into place. Verna, the woman handling the yarn with such disdain before the signing. "What were they arguing about?"

Jenika leaned closer, her voice barely audible. "I don't know all the details, but it turns out, Shanice was running a scam. The police found files on her computer showing she'd been marking up merchandise prices. The tags had the real price, but the QR codes scanned higher—just by a few cents or dollars. Most people didn't notice, but Verna caught on."

Hazel stared at Jenika, her thoughts racing. "Verna figured it out? When she came to the shop?"

"Exactly," Jenika said, nodding emphatically. "That's what the whole argument was about." She sat back, smiling as if the mystery were solved. "Now we can enjoy the retreat, knowing it's all sorted."

Jenika stood, smoothing her sweater. "Have a good class today, Hazel," she said, her tone light and breezy. She turned to leave but hesitated, pausing mid-step.

Glancing back over her shoulder, her expression softened. "And thanks again for going with me to the shop to check on Shanice," she added with a cheerful wave before walking away, her steps quick and confident.

But Hazel couldn't shake the knot of trepidation tightening in her chest. Something about this resolution felt too clean, too convenient. She watched Jenika disappear into the crowd, her cheerful demeanor in stark contrast to the tension gnawing at Hazel's gut.

She couldn't shake the nagging feeling buzzing in her mind.

This wasn't over. Not by a long shot.

The morning session passed in a haze. Hazel moved through the motions of teaching, offering polite smiles to retreat attendees and saying all the expected and proper things. But her thoughts kept returning to Verna, the argument, and the so-called resolution that everyone seemed all too eager to accept.

The news of Shanice's alleged killer spread like wildfire, shifting the retreat's mood from tense to strangely celebratory, as though solving the case erased the tragedy itself.

By lunchtime, Hazel couldn't bear the murmur of morbid speculation any longer. She needed an escape. Instead of joining the attendees for lunch, she slipped away from the hum to return to her room, craving solitude to recharge her energy and shed the exhausting mask of Whitley, her brave alter ego.

Back in the sanctuary of her room, Hazel changed into black leggings and an oversized tee, tying a silk scarf securely around her head. She sank onto the bed, exhaling deeply. For a moment, the room's quiet cocoon soothed her until her restless mind intruded once more.

The story didn't sit right. The pieces didn't fit. The timing. The details. It was all too neat, too clean.

Hazel stared at the ceiling, willing her restless thoughts to quiet. They didn't. The scene replayed in her mind on an endless loop, those gray eyes, piercing and haunting. The silence around her grew sharp, heavy, almost suffocating.

Then came a knock. Sharp. Sudden.

Hazel bolted upright, her heart hammering against her ribcage. The last thing she needed right now was a visitor.

She crept to the door, curious but cautious, and peered through the peephole. Her breath hitched.

A stranger stood on the other side. Her expression was unreadable, her striking brown eyes puffy and rimmed red from apparent crying. Long knotless blonde box braids hung down her back, tied neatly with a hand-dyed knit handkerchief at the nape of her neck.

Hazel hesitated, fingers hovering over the doorknob. Her pulse quickened, each beat echoing in her ears.

Who was this woman? And what could she possibly want?

Chapter 15: Saturday Afternoon

Another sharp knock started Hazel.

She froze, her fingers tightening around the doorknob and peered through the peephole. The woman wasn't familiar, but she didn't look entirely out of place. Her fitted hand-dyed knit sweater, mom jeans, and polished loafers gave her the look of a retreat attendee.

Maybe she just wants to follow up on something from class? But how did she find my room?

It wouldn't be the first time a student needed clarity after a session, though most stuck to questions in the lobby or dining room.

Before Hazel could mull it over, the woman knocked again, the sound reverberating through the quiet hallway.

"Yes?" Hazel opened the door a crack, her voice polite but tinged with caution. "Can I help you?"

The stranger's sharp eyes swept over Hazel, appraising her. "Are you Hazel Whitmore? The one who had the book signing at Yarn-monious?" She asked, her voice trembling with barely concealed anger. "The woman who put the noose around my mother's neck?"

Hazel's breath caught and her heart dropped as the words sank in. "Excuse me?" she finally managed, her voice barely above a whisper.

The woman didn't wait for an invitation. She pushed past Hazel into the suite, her movements brisk and deliberate. She stopped in front of the couch, placing an oversized bag on the coffee table.

Hazel stood dumbfounded in the doorway. After a beat, she closed the door and took a tentative step forward. "I'm sorry, but...what are you talking about? Who are you?" she asked, protectively crossing one arm across her body to hug herself.

The woman folded her arms tightly across her chest, as if holding herself together, bouncing one leg nervously. "My name is Shameka Shales. My mother is Verna Shales. We run Sunset Fiber Works. Maybe you've heard of us?"

Hazel nodded.

Shameka continued, her voice edged with bitterness. "Well, the police arrested my mother this morning. Detective Ridley told me it was because of your statement, something about hearing her arguing with Shanice the night of your book signing. But that's not true," she said, her words barely concealing her rage.

Hazel's heart dropped. "Wait, what? I never told them that! I didn't even know who Shanice was arguing with," she protested in defense, the full weight of Shameka's words hitting her. The woman must be mistaken and heard wrong. "All I said was that I heard voices in the back room."

"That's not what Detective Ridley said," Shameka shot back, her voice cracking. "Now my mother is sitting in a jail cell, and I don't know what to do." Her composure broke, and she looked away, tears brimming in her striking brown eyes.

Hazel felt a pang of guilt, though she knew she hadn't done anything wrong. She shuffled awkwardly before darting to the bathroom to grab a box of tissues. Returning, she handed it to Shameka.

"I'm so sorry you're going through this," Hazel said gently, her voice soft but unsure. "But...I don't know how I can help."

Sniffling, Shameka pulled herself together, dabbing at her eyes. "There's only one way to help," she said, standing abruptly. "I need to clear my mom's name. And the only way to do that is to figure out who really killed Shanice."

Hazel stared at her, speechless. "I...I don't see how that involves me."

Shameka stepped closer into Hazel's space, determination hardening her features. "You found the body. You were there. What can you tell me about the scene?"

Hazel didn't retreat from Shameka's closeness, but her stomach twisted at the memory of what she saw at Yarn-monious. "Look," she began carefully, "to be clear, I wasn't alone. Jenika asked me to go with her to check on Shanice, and we...we found her." She swallowed the lump in her throat. "There was a glass drop spindle in her neck—one of the drop spindles your mom makes. And yes, someone saw her arguing with Shanice."

Shameka flinched but didn't back down. "Was there anything unusual about the store that night? Anything that seemed out of place?"

Hazel shook her head slowly. "I wouldn't know. I'd only been there the day of my signing. Honestly, the best person to ask would be Jules or Jenika. They were both there that night."

"I've tried calling Jules. She's our main contact for inventory updates," Shameka said, her frustration evident. "I've left half a dozen messages, but she hasn't called back, and now I'm scared something's wrong."

"What about Jenika? Have you spoken to her?" Hazel asked.

"No, I don't have her contact information," Shameka admitted, her voice thick with frustration and exhaustion, the weight of mother's situation evident.

The room fell silent, the tension thick as both women seemed lost in their thoughts. Then Beyoncé's *Diva* suddenly blared from the bedroom, making Hazel jump.

"Sorry," Hazel muttered as she rushed to silence her phone alarm on the bedroom nightstand. Returning, she gestured toward her naptime outfit of a comfortable ratty old tee and leggings. "That's my alarm for my next class. I need to get ready to head back downstairs."

Reluctantly, Shameka walked toward the door, pausing with her hand on the knob. She hesitated for a moment before glancing back at Hazel, her eyes pleading.

"Can you help me, please?" she asked, her voice trembling. "I know you don't know me and it's a big ask. I'm all alone without my mom, and she won't survive in a place like that—not at her age and especially not with her medical issues."

Hazel hesitated. She closed her hands tight, her fingers digging into her palm. Every instinct screamed to stay out of it. She was no Miss Marple and no one's hero. This wasn't her problem.

But the weight of Shameka's plea struck a chord. Hazel knew all too well what it felt like to be all alone, to have no one to lean on.

Finally, she sighed. "I don't know how I can help. But I'll try. Meet me in the dining room after my last session. I'll tell you everything I remember."

Shameka's shoulders sagged with relief and tears trickled down her cheeks. "Thank you," she whispered. She opened the door and slipped out of the room, leaving Hazel alone with her thoughts.

Hazel stood there, staring at the closed door. She waited a beat, then walked over and peeked through the peephole. Shameka was retreating down the hallway, her steps slow and unsure.

Hazel leaned forward, resting her head against the cold metal door, her hands trembling. "What have I gotten myself into now?" she murmured.

She closed her eyes, drawing in a slow, deep breath to steady herself. The weight of Shameka's plea pressed heavily on her chest, concern churning in her stomach like an unrelenting tide. Her gaze dropped to her hands, shaking visibly. "Pull it together, Hazel. You can't focus on

Shameka or Verna right now. You've got a job to do," she told herself in a quiet, firm voice.

Determined to push aside her spiraling thoughts, Hazel turned her attention to the materials for her afternoon session. She sifted through her bag, organized her notes, and yarn swatches she planned to use. The morning's group of students had breezed through the standard material faster than expected, and she wanted to offer them bonus exercises; something extra to enhance their experience.

As she sorted the stack of papers and yarn swatches, her fingers brushed against a copy of her book, *Sweaters That Fit*. She hesitated, picking it up and flipping through the pages, her fingertips lingering on the familiar words.

A flood of memories, bittersweet and vivid, swept over her. The road to this moment hadn't been easy. Hazel had spent years designing patterns, pitching to publications, and collecting rejections like unwanted souvenirs. She remembered the heartbreak of being turned away over and over again. Then, just when she was ready to quit, an email she'd nearly deleted changed everything. A publisher had stumbled upon her self-published book and wanted to bring it to a broader audience.

A small, bitter smile played on her lips. She had built her success brick by brick, often with no help at all. When she'd been in the thick of it, reaching out to more established designers for guidance, she'd been met with silence—or worse. One comment still stung: *"I figured it out on my own, so you can too."* That had been the moment Hazel decided to go it alone.

No one had helped me. Why should I help anyone else?

The thought was cold, but it clung to her like a shadow. She couldn't afford to risk everything she'd worked so hard to build—not for someone she'd just met and didn't know. Hazel sighed and closed the book, pushing it aside. Stick to the plan. Teach the classes. That's what I'm here for.

Decision made, Hazel stood and began preparing for the next session. She dressed quickly, slipping into the same outfit she'd worn that morning, and gathered her materials. As she moved toward the door, Shameka's words echoed in her mind.

"The only way to clear my mom is to figure out who actually killed Shanice."

Her stomach churned. Could Shameka be right? Had Hazel unwittingly played a part in Verna's arrest? She hadn't mentioned any names to the police. The only people who would know who was in the back room with Shanice were Jules and Jenika. Maybe she'd have to ask them about it—carefully.

Hazel shook her head, trying to push the thought aside. Focus on the class. Deal with Shameka later.

She checked her bag one last time. Confirming she had everything she needed, she stepped out into the hallway, and the door clicked closed behind her. The metallic ding of the elevator echoed faintly as she walked toward it. Her thoughts raced relentlessly as she pressed the button and waited.

By the time Hazel reached the classroom, she had stuffed her uneasiness into a neat little box at the back of her mind. Whitley was in charge now, the braver, more confident version of herself that helped her navigate these events.

Hazel stepped inside and scanned the room. As the students began filtering in, she focused on setting up the extra materials. But as she arranged the bonus materials, her thoughts kept drifting back to Shameka's desperate plea—and to Verna, sitting in a cold, sterile cell somewhere, accused of a crime Hazel wasn't sure she'd committed.

The juxtaposition was jarring. Shameka's tear-streaked face contrasted starkly with the happy smiling faces of the retreat attendees. As Hazel greeted her students and began the lesson, a new determination settled in her chest. She had to figure out who was responsible for Shanice's untimely death.

Chapter 16: Saturday Evening

The day's classes had ended, leaving the attendees visibly drained as they shuffled back to their rooms to rest before the evening banquet. Hazel, equally exhausted, entered the dining room, craving a moment of quiet before the bustle resumed. Her gaze swept the room and landed on Shameka, seated in a corner, hunched over a chaotic stack of papers. How long had she been sitting here?

The gentle clatter of silverware and murmurs of staff setting up the buffet filled the air. Hazel hesitated, her hand tightening on the strap of her bag. She wasn't sure what to say or if she even wanted to say anything. But there was no turning back now. Shameka had seen her and waved weakly in acknowledgment.

"Hi," Hazel greeted awkwardly, sliding into the seat across from her.

Shameka offered a small smile but quickly dropped her gaze back to the papers, her hands trembling as she shuffled through the pages.

For a moment, the only sounds between them were the faint rustle of Shameka flipping through the papers and the clinking of water glasses being filled nearby. Then, without notice or explanation, Shameka pushed a sheet of paper across the table at Hazel.

"Read this," she said, pointing to a section at the bottom. "It's from the notes my mother's lawyer sent me. It's all they're using to charge her."

Hazel picked up the photocopied sheet. The handwriting was hurried, as if the note-taker had been racing to keep up. At the top of the paper in bold letters was written 'PRELIMINARY OBSERVATIONS - FULL AUTOPSY TO FOLLOW IN A FEW DAYS - CORONER'S OFFICE BACKED UP'.

Shameka leaned over and tapped the text at the bottom of the page, her voice trembling as she explained, "It says Shanice's time of death was around 10 p.m. Penetrated neck wound with a glass drop spindle."

Hazel's breath caught at the brutal simplicity of the description. "And based on this, they think your mom...?"

"She didn't do it" Shameka's voice cracked. "She wasn't even at the shop then. After the argument with Shanice, she called me. She always goes to her favorite spot at the park when she's upset—to think things through. That's where she was until almost midnight."

"Do the police know this?" Hazel asked gently.

Shameka nodded, her face shadowed with frustration. "Mom told them she wasn't there after the book signing ended, but there's no proof. No one saw her at the park. And the police...they don't care. Detective Ridley is calling this case closed so he can retire with a clean record. No open investigation," she said cynically, anger flashing in her eyes like twin flames. "He just wants to see somebody, anybody, charged. And unfortunately, he found a scapegoat, my mother. She's just convenient."

Hazel listened, unsure what to say. Her mind spun with the information. Did she believe Shameka? Was she looking for a scapegoat, someone else to blame, in place of her mother?

"Jenika and Jules are both still not responding to my calls," Shameka said, her voice pleading like she was about to cry. "I feel like one, or both, of them knows something and have answers to so many of my questions," she said with a whine in her voice. She flipped through a few more pages. "Look at this...right here." She pushed another page forward, her hands trembling.

Hazel took the page and read the section marked. It was a partial transcript of Jenika's statement to Detective Ridley:

Stevenson: I heard shouting coming from the back room that Shanice used as an office and extra storage space. It wasn't the first time I'd heard Shanice shouting at someone, so I thought nothing of it. I assumed from the voices that it was still Verna in there with Shanice, or maybe Jules. They've been known to go a round or two with each other. After Hazel left, I left right after too. The voices were still in there.

Ridley: You left her in a shouting match? Weren't you worried for Shanice?

Stevenson: Like I said, Shanice argues with a lot of people. I didn't think much of it. I didn't think whoever was in there would kill her.

Ridley: Do you recognize this? I'm showing Miss Stevenson a photo.

Stevenson: Yes.

Ridley: For the tape, can you tell me what it is?

Stevenson: It's a handmade glass drop spindle, a new product we recently started carrying. It's the only one like it around. They are one-of-a-kind.

Ridley: Who made the drop spindle?

Stevenson: Verna, the owner of Sunset Fiber Works makes them exclusively for Yarn-monious. That's one of hers.

The words felt heavy in Hazel's hand. She quickly scanned down the page. Here eye caught something:

Stevenson: Shanice and Jules argued a lot. I didn't think anything of it.
Ridley: What was the argument about?
Stevenson: I honestly don't know.

Shameka stared intently into Hazel's eyes, willing her to understand, to see the connection.

After a beat, she snatched the piece of paper back and replaced it with another. "And then, there's a note here," she said in a rush, buzzing with adrenaline and pointed to a passage not yet highlighted, "that reports that the fingerprints on the drop spindle belonged to my mother," Shameka added, her voice rising in frustration. "That's all they needed, apparently. Never mind that it's *her* drop spindle. She made it. Of course, her fingerprints are on it!"

Shameka's hands shook violently. She dropped her head onto her crossed arms on the tabletop and broke into sobs.

Hazel froze, her mind racing, unsure of what to do. Her eyes darted around the room, desperate for help, but the staff setting up the buffet were oblivious. Awkwardly, she rose and grabbed a handful of napkins from the utensil counter.

"Here," she said softly, holding them out.

Shameka lifted her head, her face blotchy and tear-streaked. She accepted a napkin with a whispered thanks and dabbed at her swollen eyes.

Hazel sat back down, her heart twisting painfully. She didn't want to be here, caught in the middle of this tangled mess. She didn't want to get involved. She'd worked so hard to build her life alone, without help. The idea of risking everything for a stranger is unbearable.

But Shameka's eyes...the pain in them was too familiar. Hazel saw the same fear she had lived with for so long, the same gnawing loneliness. She grappled with the idea of what would happen if she crumbled and not having anyone there to put the pieces back together.

Can she afford to help Shameka? Is she strong enough to build herself back up if it all came crashing down?

Her mind drifted to why she'd written *Sweaters That Fit* in the first place. It had been her way of giving others the guidance she'd desperately needed when she first started out and was struggling. And though the journey had been lonely and full of obstacles, she'd found community along the way. There was a softening that happened within her, after years of building up walls, when she put herself out there to support crocheters and knitters build their confidence. Maybe...just maybe.

Hazel took a deep breath, her resolve wavering.

"I'll help," she heard herself say, the words surprising even her as they slipped out almost involuntarily. "But I don't know what I can do. I'm only here for a few more days."

Shameka's head shot up, her eyes flickering with a spark of hope. "Really?"

"Yes. Really." Hazel wasn't entirely sure why she said it, but she couldn't ignore the pull to help. Something in Shameka's desperation made it impossible to walk away. She glanced at the teetering stack of papers Shameka had brought over, chaos and urgency spilling across the table. There was no turning back now. "So, where do we start?"

Before Shameka could respond, KNote stormed over to their table, her steps sharp and deliberate. She was dressed in fitted blue jeans and a plain black tee, topped with the same sweater her mom wore the day of the book signing. Tears streamed down her face, her red-rimmed eyes locked onto Shameka with a look of fury.

"Your mother killed my mom," KNote spat, her voice trembling with a volatile mix of anger and grief. "And now I have no one. I'm all alone."

Her knees buckled, and she collapsed onto the floor, her sobs tearing through the room like a jagged wound.

Hazel froze, KNote's words slamming into her chest, leaving her breathless. The room seemed to shrink, the weight of her pain was suffocating. Hazel's gaze flicked between KNote, a shattered girl sobbing at her feet, whose mother had been viciously murdered, and Shameka, frozen in silent torment, her mother now accused of a crime that could destroy them both.

A hundred questions raced through Hazel's mind, colliding in a storm of disbelief and dread. But only one rose above the rest, chilling her to the core that mattered now: What terrible secret bound their mothers together?

Awkwardly, Hazel knelt beside KNote, rubbing her shuddering back, her sobs breaking into hiccups. The raw grief in her cries tugged at something deep within Hazel—a fierce resolve she hadn't felt in years. Someone had murdered KNote's mother, Shanice Keller, a legend both on the stage and in the fiber world. Hazel's heart clenched as she thought of the vibrant woman, so beloved, so full of life. But why? Who could have hated her enough to end it so viciously?

Questions gnawed at her. Was the killer someone from Shanice's storied music career, where old rivalries and buried secrets could simmer for decades? Or had the answer spun itself into the tight-knit fabric of the fiber arts community Shanice had adored?

Hazel didn't know where to begin, but as she looked at the two women—one mourning a mother gone forever, the other desperate to save hers—she knew she had to try. There was no turning back now.

Chapter 17: Saturday Evening

The lobby buzzed with energy as retreat attendees gathered for the banquet. Hazel's stomach churned at the smell of the variety of food wading through the air. Conversations mingled with the ding of elevators, spilling a cacophony of voices and laughter into the previously quiet space. Excited chatter filled the air, a stark contrast to Hazel's somber mood. How could they act so carefree, so joyous, as if Shanice's death hadn't shaken their community just days ago?

Frustration simmered beneath Hazel's surface. She stood abruptly, her chair scraping against the polished floor. Shameka and KNote flinched at the sudden motion. Realizing their startled reactions, Hazel eased back into her seat, forcing a calm she didn't feel, her voice softer but firm.

"We should probably find somewhere quieter to talk," she said, scanning the room as the sounds of the crowd grew louder. "The banquet crowd will be coming through here soon."

Both women nodded in agreement.

"Where can we go?" Shameka asked, glancing at KNote, whose red-rimmed eyes revealed her exhaustion.

Hazel hesitated, then offered, "My suite upstairs has a couch and a dining table. We can talk there."

The trio rose without another word and left the dining room, weaving through the growing crowd. Hazel kept her head down, determined to avoid unnecessary interactions. But fate had other plans.

"Hazel!"

The voice called from across the lobby, clear and insistent. Hazel winced, her pace quickening.

"Hazel!" The voice rang out louder, closer.

Reluctantly, she stopped and turned. A striking figure hurried toward her, their Icelandic crochet sweater in earthy tones cinched at the waist over a dramatic taffeta skirt. Chunky platform boots added inches to their petite frame. As they closed the distance, Hazel couldn't help but notice their flawless skin and perfectly manicured mustache, vivid brown eyes framed by long lashes, perfectly arched brows, and a swipe of green eyeshadow that matched their nail polish. The stranger came to a stop, breathless but beaming.

"Hi! My name is Ivy," they said, their voice warm and lilting. "I was supposed to be in today's class, but I wasn't feeling well."

Instinctively, Hazel took a small step back, wary of catching whatever illness Ivy might have.

Ivy caught the movement and chuckled softly. "Oh, no, Girl. It's nothing like that," they reassured her with a conspiratorial grin. "I was just...hungover." Leaning in, they whispered, "Some of us went out last night, and, well, I did too much," they said and pointed to a group standing together across the lobby chatting.

They giggled, covering their mouth with a delicate hand, their demeanor radiating mischief.

"Anyway," Ivy continued, straightening up, "I just wanted to say how much you've inspired me. Your book changed everything for me. I used to feel so out of place in this community. I couldn't find sweaters that fit my style or my build. But your book taught me how to create clothes that feel like *me*. And look!"

They twirled with a flourish, pinching the hem of their sweater, and ended in an exaggerated curtsy.

Hazel's heart swelled as tears pricked her eyes. "That's amazing, Ivy," she said sincerely, her voice thick with emotion. "I am so proud of you. You did this. You made it yours." She emphasized the last word, wanting Ivy to know the accomplishment was theirs to celebrate.

Ivy's eyes sparkled. "You don't know what it means to me." With another twirl, Ivy said, "I feel like I've emerged from a drab cocoon, and now I'm a beautiful little butterfly—confident, stylish, and so *me*."

Hazel grinned, her heart swelling. "I don't want to keep you," they said, eyeing Shameka and KNote huddled in a corner obviously waiting for Hazel. "May I hug you?" Ivy asked.

Though not typically a hugger, Hazel found herself nodding. They embraced warmly, Ivy's gratitude etched into Hazel's mind.

"Thank you for being you, for being here, and sharing your story. It means everything." Hazel said as they broke apart.

Hazel watched Ivy walk away and felt a flicker of warmth amidst the cold weight of Shanice's death. This was why she did what she did—to help people rediscover themselves. She loved helping people even though she'd been hurt in the past. And now, she'd do everything she could to find the truth for KNote and Shameka.

Hazel turned to rejoin Shameka and KNote by the elevators. She was more than convinced she needed to do whatever she could to help them figure out who killed Shanice and set Verna free. Together, they ascended to her suite, each woman silent and lost in their own thoughts.

In the quiet living area, dimly lit by soft lamp lights, the early evening already dark, the tension returned, heavy and unspoken. They sat around the table, the weight of their task settling over them.

KNote broke the silence, her voice raw and trembling. "Do you really think Verna's innocent?" Her gaze shifted from Hazel toward Shameka, suspicion and grief etched into her face.

Shameka straightened her spine, her jaw tightening. "Yes," she said with force. "My mother didn't do this. She's stubborn, sure, and sharp-tongued. But a murderer? No."

KNote's lip quivered. She gripped the table's edge, a single tear slipping down her cheek unchecked. Her voice broke, trembling as she whispered, "If it wasn't Verna, then...who else could've done this?" She asked, her voice full of emotion and accusation.

Hazel leaned forward, her voice calm but resolute. "That's what we're going to find out."

The words hung in the air, fragile yet galvanizing. Shameka nodded, her eyes glistening with a faint hope. KNote remained silent, her doubt lingering.

Hazel's mind raced to connect the pieces as she mentally unraveled the fragments of information Shameka shared earlier. The glass spindle. The argument. The fingerprints. Everything seemed to point to Shameka's mother—or perhaps it was designed to.

"We need to start with Shanice's timeline," Hazel said, opening her notebook with a pen poised, her tone taking on a sharper edge. "What time did she leave the shop that night?"

"Around 9 o'clock," Shameka answered. "That's when my mom left for the park. She called me as she was leaving."

"Was she upset?"

Shameka hesitated. "Yes. She and Shanice had been arguing earlier, but she didn't say what about. Just that it was over something business related."

"Business related? You're business partners...she didn't tell you?" Hazel asked, jotting the words down.

"She said she'd handle it and tell me later."

Hazel made a note in her notebook. "And you have no idea what it could be about?"

"No idea," Shameka admitted.

Hazel turned to KNote. "Do you have any idea what their disagreement might have been about?"

KNote shook her head. "None. I don't pay attention to stuff like that at the shop. Maybe I should have," she said, hanging her head in guilt.

Hazel's attention returned to Shameka. "What about the drop spindle? Why would anyone use that as a weapon? It seems...deliberate, like they wanted to frame Verna."

"It's unique," KNote said quietly. Both Hazel and Shameka turned to her in surprise. She swallowed hard, brushing away a stray tear. "The spindle. My mom told me about it. It's one of Verna's custom designs. She only made a handful of them, and they're not easy to find. Whoever used it...they knew exactly what they were doing."

Hazel's pen stilled mid-note. "Do you think it could have been someone from the fiber community? Someone who knew about Verna's work? Or was it used because it was there and convenient?"

KNote shrugged, her shoulders sagging. "Maybe the fiber world. Or it could've been someone from the music world. My mom was not always easy to get along with."

Shameka bristled. "What's that supposed to mean?"

"It means she had enemies," KNote snapped, her grief flashing into anger. "There are a lot of people who didn't like her. And maybe your mom was one of them!"

"Stop." Hazel's voice cut through the tension like a knife. Both women looked at her, startled.

"Arguing about this isn't going to help. If we want answers, we need to work together." Hazel's voice softened.

KNote folded her arms but said nothing. Shameka gave a reluctant nod.

Hazel tapped her pen against the table, her mind piecing together a plan. "Here's what we do. We need to dig deeper into Shanice's life—her relationships, her enemies, her secrets. Someone out there knows something."

She looked at KNote as she continued. "We'll go to the shop tonight to see if we can find any clues that might help us."

Knote gave a firm nod, determination flickering in her red-rimmed eyes.

Hazel shifted her gaze to Shameka. "And you need to talk to your mom. Find out what that argument with Shanice was really about. What was so serious that it led to a shouting match?"

Shameka straightened, her expression resolute. "We need to talk to Jules and Jenika too," she added, her voice sharper now. "I'm convinced they're hiding something. Something that could put all the pieces together. Jenika knows more than what she told Detective Ridley in her interview."

Hazel nodded. "I agreed. Once you're done, meet us at the shop."

The resolve in her own voice surprised herself. Hazel hadn't come to this retreat planning to play detective, but here she was, caught up in a whirlwind of murder, lies, and heartbreak.

They had a plan of action. It wasn't perfect, but at least it was a place to start. Hazel had arrived at this retreat intending to keep her head down, focus on her classes, and stay out of everyone's way. Yet, here she was, drawn into the lives of these two women, their pain and determination pulling her far out of her comfort zone.

As the three women sat together in the dimly lit hotel suite, the weight of the task ahead settled heavily in the air. Hazel looked at the women, their faces etched with worry and hope.

She let out a slow breath. The threads of this mystery felt impossibly tangled and messy, but if there was one thing Hazel knew how to do, it was untangling knots.

Somewhere within this mess of lies and secrets, the truth was waiting to be uncovered.

A killer was hiding, and Hazel was ready to unravel every thread until the truth was laid bare.

Chapter 18: Saturday Evening

The evening air bit at Hazel and KNote as they stepped out of the car in the dimly lit Municipal Parking Lot. A gust of cold wind rustled the bare branches overhead, sending a shiver down Hazel's spine. They walked briskly toward Yarn-monious, the looming storefront illuminated by soft, golden light spilling from the windows.

Hazel paused in her tracks, taken aback. "The lights are on?" she said, half to herself.

KNote nodded, pulling her jacket tighter around her. "Jules texted me earlier," she explained. "She and some of the staff are here cleaning up. The police left quite a mess, fingerprint dust everywhere. They want everything ready for tomorrow."

Tomorrow—the retreat's class-free day when attendees would flood the shop, eager to browse and buy yarn. This would be the last event before the retreat wrap-up. The idea of cheerful shoppers laughing and chatting, filing in the very space that had witnessed Shanice's brutal murder made Hazel's stomach turn.

At the door, KNote hesitated, her hand hovering just above the handle.

Hazel placed a reassuring hand on her arm. "It's okay," she said gently, though her voice wavered.

Inside, the scene was unexpectedly lively. Staff members moved around, each engrossed in tasks: dusting shelves, restocking displays, rearranging furniture, and tidying up. The air smelled faintly of lavender cleaning products, and a faint hum of chatter filled the space, adding to the bustling atmosphere.

"Good evening," came a voice from nearby. An older woman with a mop in hand smiled warmly at them.

"Suki," KNote acknowledged with a faint smile, her tone soft but steady. "Is Jules around?"

"Yeah, she's over..." Suki gestured toward a table at the back of the shop. "She was just over there a moment ago straightening up the yarn," she said, a note of uncertainty crept into her voice.

Hazel and KNote followed Suki's gesture toward the back, but Jules was nowhere in sight.

"She must have stepped out through the back," Suki offered hesitantly.

Hazel scanned the room, her frown deepening as questions swirled in her mind. Where is Jules? Why isn't she here as she promised? Is she avoiding KNote? Or is something else going on? All these thoughts ran through Hazel's mind, colliding as they tried to make sense.

"Thanks, Suki," KNote replied, a hint of disappointment in her voice. Then, louder, she addressed the room. "Thank you all for your hard work tonight."

The staff looked up, nodding or offering faint smiles before returning to their tasks. Hazel noticed how much KNote had matured from the spoiled brat she'd first met only days ago. Has it really only been two days? Hazel wondered. So much has happened. It feels like weeks.

Hazel followed KNote toward the back room. As they neared the room, a wave of nausea washed over her. Her breath hitched as memories from her last visit clawed their way to the surface: the blood, the vacant eyes, the police tape, the unshakable smell of despair.

KNote reached the door first, her hand trembling as it closed around the handle. She froze, the weight of the moment pressing down on her like an anchor.

A gasp from behind startled Hazel. She turned to see Suki frozen in place, mop forgotten in hand, watching KNote with wide eyes. Around the room, other staff members had stopped what they were doing, their gazes fixed on KNote standing at the threshold.

Steeling herself, KNote straightened her spine, pushed the door open, and stepped inside. Hazel followed closely, her protective instincts kicking in.

The lights flickered on, revealing a jarring sight. The room was in disarray. While the storage shelves and supplies appeared untouched, the desk drawers had been yanked open, their contents spilled across the floor. Papers, receipts, and scraps of yarn littered the space in chaotic confusion.

"What a mess," KNote muttered, her voice strained. "Did the police really leave it like this?"

Hazel's eyes narrowed as she surveyed the room. Something about the scene felt...wrong. The chaos wasn't random; it had a deliberate, searching quality. But she kept her thoughts to herself, not wanting to alarm KNote.

"Let's get this cleaned up," Hazel said, forcing a note of calm into her voice. "Maybe we'll find something important." Or discover whatever the person who made this mess was looking for, she thought to herself.

They worked in silence, sorting through the mess. Hazel crouched near the desk and picked up the wire trash can and began tossing the discarded papers back in. Her fingers brushed against something hard and smooth beneath the chair—a small plastic tube.

Frowning, Hazel held it up to the light, trying to determine its purpose. It didn't seem to belong to anything in the room. Shrugging, she slipped it into her pocket and resumed tidying.

After nearly half an hour, the room was back in order.

"Did you find anything useful?" Hazel asked, dusting off her hands.

KNote wiped her hands on her jeans and sighed. "Nothing. If there was anything important here, my mom would have put it in her safe."

"A safe?" Hazel echoed, glancing around. "I didn't see one," Hazel said, looking around the room.

"Yeah," KNote's lips curving into a small, sly smile. "Follow me. If there were any important documents or anything like that, they'd be in there."

She walked to the far wall and lifted a painting from its hook. Behind it, the drywall was uneven, a subtle square indentation visible in the plaster. With practiced ease, KNote pressed on one side, and the panel popped free to reveal a small black safe.

"Clever." Hazel raised an eyebrow.

KNote placed the panel on the floor, leaning it against the wall. She stood before the safe, her fingers deftly turning the dial. The lock clicked, and the door swung open, revealing a neat stack of cash, a bundle of documents, and a small collection of photographs.

KNote carefully removed the contents, spreading them out on the table. As she sifted through the photos, one caught her attention. Her brow furrowed. The image showed Shanice, much younger and smiling, cradling a baby.

KNote stared at the photo for a long moment. She flipped it over, then handed it to Hazel. "Look at this," she said. "That's my mom when she was much younger."

Hazel took the photo and looked. Handing it back, she said, "Oh, you were so cute."

A shadow crossed KNote's face. She didn't take the photo. "Yeah, cute baby, but...that's not me," she whispered, her voice shaky.

She turned the photo over in Hazel's hand to show the scrawled words on the back: 'My baby, Lyrix.'

"That's not me," she repeated, almost to herself.

Hazel studied the photo closer. KNote was right; that was a different baby. The nose was similar. The hair was different, but that can change. But the eyes...the baby had bright gray eyes, so different from KNote's deep brown ones.

Something tinkled in the back of her mind. It was something important, but it was too far out of reach to grab. Like a butterfly, the niggling thought fluttered away.

"Who is this baby?" Hazel asked softly.

KNote shook her head, her voice tinged with disbelief. "I have no idea. The writing on the back says, 'My baby, Lyrix,' so it's my mom's baby. But I have no idea who it is or if they are still alive or dead. She never told me she had a baby before me," KNote said, her voice filled with anger, worry, and confusion.

"What does this mean?" KNote's voice cracked with anguish. "Did my mom have another child? Why didn't she ever tell me?"

Hazel reached out, placing a comforting hand on KNote's shoulder. "I don't know," she said gently. "But we'll figure it out. This might be a piece of the puzzle. We just need to figure out where it fits."

"Do you think it has anything to do with her murder?" KNote asked, her voice trembling as unshed tears shimmered in her eyes.

Hazel hesitated, a knot tightening in her chest. "Maybe," she said cautiously, her tone measured. "I don't know. But we're going to find out." Her words carried a steady reassurance, though a flicker of doubt lingered.

The mystery surrounding Shanice's death was growing murkier and more twisted with each passing moment. Every answer only revealed more questions. Hazel knew they were far from unraveling the tangled threads of this case. But now, they had another thread to pull that Hazel was determined to untangle.

Chapter 19: Still Saturday Evening

The air in the shop felt heavier as Hazel and KNote emerged from the back office, their earlier discovery leaving a cloud of unanswered questions. They settled into the cozy nook near the front, the warmth of the space contrasting sharply with the chill in their thoughts. Yarn-monious, typically alive with laughter and chatter, was eerily silent now. The cleanup crew had finished and left, locking the front door behind them, leaving only the faint scent of lavender soap and wool lingering in the air.

The shop was ready. Tomorrow, retreat attendees would flood the shop for the planned shopping spree, their excitement likely unshaken by the tragedy. But Hazel's mind was far from peaceful.

A sharp knock at the locked door startled them both. Hazel and KNote exchanged a glance before KNote moved to the door.

Shameka stood outside, her face pale and drawn, her red-rimmed eyes betraying hours of crying.

KNote quickly unlocked the door and stepped aside as Shameka entered. Exhaustion clung to her like a heavy cloak, her movements sluggish. She held out a take-out bag toward KNote. "The delivery guy showed up just as I arrived," she said, her voice barely above a murmur.

KNote took the bag and led the way back to the nook, her voice softening. "I ordered dinner for us from the Ethiopian place down the street. I wasn't sure what you'd like, so I got a mix of spicy, mild, meat, and vegan, so you will have your choice. I hope that's okay?" She gave a faint smile. "Oh, and there are utensils too."

Together, Hazel and KNote helped unpack the containers, spreading out the colorful dishes on the small table. The aroma of warm spices filled the air, momentarily lifting the heaviness that settled over them.

Shameka sank into a chair, her shoulders slumping under an invisible weight. She said nothing, her gaze fixed on the table but unfocused, lost in thought.

Hazel and KNote exchanged a glance before taking their seats.

Shameka drew a deep breath, her voice raw as she finally spoke. "I talked to my mom." Her voice cracked. "She's not doing well. She's not eating. She looks so...frail. My mom is the strongest person I know but..." She faltered, a single tear escaping down her cheek before she quickly brushed it away. Shameka inhaled deeply, visibly forcing herself to continue. "...this person does not resemble that woman I know. She told me about the argument with Shanice."

Hazel and KNote leaned in, their attention unwavering.

"For the past few weeks," Shameka swallowed hard, gathering her thoughts, "there's been talk among other vendors about shady dealings at the shop. My mom's in a mastermind group with other fiber artists who sell their work here on consignment. A few of them noticed discrepancies in their sales reports, like missing items or lower payouts than expected. One even said a customer told them they were overcharged at checkout."

"Overcharged how?" Hazel asked, frowning. She absently picked at a piece of injera, its tangy flavor barely registering as she processed Shameka's words.

"Mom started hearing these rumblings after we agreed to the trunk show," Shameka continued. "She didn't want to believe anything was wrong—she's worked with Shanice for years, since the shop opened. She decided to come down at the last minute to see for herself. She didn't want me to come because she didn't know what she'd find. When she got here, she noticed something strange. Some of the yarn had strange QR codes that scanned at higher prices than the tags showed."

KNote folded her arms defensively. "Retailers set their own prices. Why would that be an issue?" The words rang hollow even as she said them.

"It's an issue, especially if the product is on consignment," Shameka explained, "because the seller and the shop agree beforehand on the price and the percentage of sales each will receive. And it's worse if the tagged price and the scanned price don't match. Changing it is deceptive."

KNote bristled, her voice rising. "My mom would never cheat her customers. I've helped with inventory and sales, and I've never seen anything shady going on."

Hazel raised a hand, mediating. "Is there a way we can check this out now? Let's test a few skeins," she suggested.

A discrepancy like this could be a simple oversight—or a deliberate act. Either way, they needed proof before jumping to conclusions.

They cleaned their hands and headed to the cashier's desk. They moved past towering shelves of yarn, their footsteps echoing in the now empty shop.

KNote grabbed two skeins, one from the trunk show display and another from a shelf marked Local Dyers, and scanned the first yarn's QR code. The screen displayed a price higher than the tag, followed by an error message.

Without reading it, KNote instinctively pressed "OK."

KNote's face tightened as she scanned the next yarn. The error message flashed again, and her finger hovered over the "OK" button.

"Wait. Don't clear it yet," Hazel said sharply. "What does the error message actually say?"

They all leaned in closer to read the error message carefully. It was confusing, filled with technical jargon, but at the bottom, there was a tiny line of text. An unfamiliar email address.

"That's not the shop's email," KNote said, her voice tinged with distress. "I know my mom," she said. "Everything was aboveboard, but this unfamiliar email..." her voice trailed off.

"Do you have access to the sales records from the night of the book signing?" Hazel asked, her mind racing.

It was a busy night. She recalled many of the attendees purchasing copies of her books to sign and enough yarn to make multiple sweaters from the book. Many shoppers wouldn't notice a few dollars higher on their receipt.

KNote nodded. "I can pull them up in the office. Why?"

"I want to test a theory," Hazel responded as they headed to the back office.

Back in the office, the atmosphere was tense as they crowded around the computer. KNote sat in the chair behind the desk and logged into the sales system, navigating to the records for the night of the signing. The numbers appeared on the screen, and all three women gasped.

"No," KNote whispered, shaking her head. "These numbers can't be right." She leaned back in the chair, her face pale. "Mom said the place was packed. There's proof on her social media pages. How could there have been so few sales? There's no way these numbers are real." She glanced at the screen, hoping for an easy explanation, but the numbers refused to lie. Her hands trembled as she thought of her mother, picturing her seated at this very desk. Was it possible her mom had missed something, or worse, turned a blind eye?

Shameka leaned closer, her voice soft but steady. "Maybe it's just a glitch in the system," she said, giving it the benefit of the doubt.

Hazel wasn't convinced. "Let's pull up another date—a time period you know for sure had a lot of activity," she suggested.

KNote nodded, though hesitation lingered in her movements. She clicked to retrieve another set of sales data. Her heart sank as the numbers appeared: equally grim. Her hands trembled as she clicked through more dates. Each one showed the same dismal trend. "These numbers aren't enough to keep the shop running, let alone pay the staff. This *has* to be an error," she said, her voice cracking.

Hazel's brow furrowed, her gaze narrowing on the screen. "I don't know...this doesn't feel like a glitch. Could someone be skimming from the shop? Maybe that's what the error messages at the cash desk are about."

"But who?" KNote's voice broke, the words coming out in a whisper. "And why didn't my mom catch this?"

KNote swallowed hard, ready to defend her mom, to push back against any implication of negligence or wrongdoing. But the mounting evidence was like quicksand, dragging her deeper into doubt.

Hazel studied KNote, a range of emotions crossing her face. She had been blindsided, Hazel thought.

"I hate to even suggest this without concrete proof," Shameka said softly, "but it would have to be someone with access. A staff member."

"Absolutely not," KNote exclaimed. "Everyone who works at Yarn-monious are good and honest people. It must be someone from her entertainment days. I've worked side-by-side with all these women, and I trust them."

The room fell silent, the weight of Shameka's words settling over them, heavy in the air.

Hazel stared at the screen and her mind raced. The numbers, the error messages, the nagging feeling she'd had ever since they started investigating—it all hinted at something more insidious. "It looks like these discrepancies have been happening for a while. Has your mom mentioned any financial issues or money troubles recently?"

KNote paused, racking her memory. "No, not that I can think of...wait. Maybe. A couple of weeks ago, I asked Mom for extra money.

It was more than my monthly allowance for a last-minute trip to Jamaica. She snapped at me, going off about everyone taking advantage and sucking her dry. She apologized later and gave me the money, but it wasn't like her. I just figured she was stressed about planning the retreat and book signing." She lowered her head, shame tugging at her voice. "I should have pressed her to learn more. I should have done more to help at the shop."

"You couldn't have known," Hazel reassured her, though doubt gnawed at her.

KNote's hands clenched into fists, her nails biting into her palms. "If someone was stealing from my mom, maybe she found out who and they killed her to cover it all up. I have to find out who."

The words tumbled out of KNote with conviction, but even as she spoke, Hazel felt a chilling thought crept in: What if it's more complicated than that? What if Shanice knew? Or worse, what if...she allowed it?

Hazel shook her head, forcing the thought away. She *couldn't* believe that—she wouldn't. Follow the facts. Don't jump to conclusions, she told herself.

Hazel placed a hand on KNote's shoulder. "We'll figure this out together," she said, steady and sure, though uncertainty twisted in her stomach. She couldn't let KNote see her own doubts, not now.

Shameka nodded. "Whoever it is, they won't get away with it," she vowed.

They both needed this mystery solved. Shameka needed to get her mother out of jail and clear her name doing whatever it took to accomplish that. KNote needed justice.

But Hazel couldn't shake the nagging feeling that they were missing something...something critical. Whoever was behind this wasn't just skimming money. They were covering their tracks and leaving a trail of chaos and distrust in their wake.

"Let's see what else the bank records show," Shameka suggested, her voice measured as she refocused the group.

As they scanned receipts and reports, a pattern emerged. A single payment of $1,111 appeared, followed by another exactly seven days later. And another. KNote's eyes widened as she traced the line of canceled checks, each made out to cash.

"What do you think this means?" Hazel asked, leaning in.

Their earlier confidence had unraveled like a dropped stitch, leaving them downcast and exhausted. The weight of everything they'd learned seemed heavier than ever, pressing them into a tense silence.

Shameka's face darkened. "Those payments are like clockwork. And they go out every week for the past three months. It looks like blackmail."

Chapter 20: Much Later Saturday Evening

The office fell silent, the weight of the word settled over them like a heavy fog. *Blackmail.* Hazel, KNote, and Shameka stepped away from the desk and returned to the nook, the remnants of dinner now cold on the table. The cozy space, with its yarn-lined walls and soft lighting, offered little comfort against the storm of questions swirling in their minds.

The mysteries surrounding Shanice's murder, the shop's sales discrepancies, and now this new twist were tangled threads in an ever-expanding web. Would they be able to unravel it before it was too late? Hazel feared they were just getting started.

The sharp sound of a ringing shattered the stillness, making all three women jump.

KNote fumbled in her bag for her phone. Her heart skipped a beat when she saw the name on the screen: Detective Ridley.

"Why is he calling so late?" she murmured, her voice trembling as she answered.

"Hello?"

"Miss Keller? This is Detective Ridley from STMPD. Are you able to talk?" His voice was brusque, but an uncharacteristic undertone made her stomach tighten.

"Yes, Detective. I can talk," she replied, glancing nervously at Hazel and Shameka. Her voice was soft and brittle. Hazel moved closer, perched on the armrest of KNote's chair, she placed a steadying hand on her shoulder.

"I'm at Yarn-monious with two friends. Do you mind if I put you on speakerphone?" KNote asked, her voice quaking. She couldn't bear the idea of hearing this alone, or worse, having to repeat it later.

The tension in the room thickened. All three women knew a call from Detective Ridley could only mean trouble.

Detective Ridley hesitated for a brief moment, then grunted. "Go ahead."

KNote tapped the screen and held out the phone on her open palm.

"We just received the final report from the coroner's office," Detective Ridley began, his words measured. "The cause of death is not what we initially thought."

KNote's breath hitched. Hazel's hand tightened on her shoulder, offering what little comfort she could.

Detective Ridley continued, his words layman but deliberate. "Your mother was stabbed with the drop spindle, as we saw, but that wasn't what killed her. The actual cause of death was an overdose of morphine. The substance was found in her stomach contents and a needle mark on her neck. The spindle was used in an attempt to obscure the injection site."

KNote stared at the phone, her face pale and stricken, her hand trembling. The words hung in the air like an echo.

"What...what does that mean?" she stammered, her wide eyes darting to between Hazel and Shameka, silently pleading.

Hazel stared at the phone, her brain working furiously to connect the information the detective was providing.

"The morphine was ingested earlier, likely during dinner," Detective Ridley explained. "And then later, she was given a fatal injection. Once she died, the killer staged the scene with the spindle to mislead us. That's why there wasn't as much blood as we'd expect from such a wound."

The room seemed to tilt. KNote listened quietly, her breathing turned shallow. Shameka gasped, her hand flying to her mouth. Hazel contemplated what this implied for Verna and their investigation.

"This shifts the focus of the investigation. We'll be in touch tomorrow with more information." Detective Ridley added matter-of-fact, his voice free of emotions.

The line clicked off, leaving a deafening silence.

Without a word, KNote dropped the phone and bolted to the bathroom. The door slammed shut, and moments later, the sound of retching filled the air.

Hazel and Shameka exchanged a glance before rushing after her. Hazel knocked gently. "KNote, dear, are you okay?"

There was no immediate response. "Can I come in? Do you need help?" she asked.

The toilet flushed, and the faucet hissed.

"Just...just give me a second," KNote's faint voice came through the door.

"All right. We're here if you need us. Just give a shout if you need anything." Hazel said, her voice soft with concern.

The two women returned to the nook, their expressions grim.

"What does this mean?" Shameka asked, breaking the silence. "Is my mom getting out of jail?" She winced, guilt flickering across her face. "I mean...I want her free, but Shanice is still gone. KNote's mom is still gone."

Hazel didn't respond immediately, her thoughts racing. Morphine? A needle? Who would have access to those? And why? This changes everything. The new information opened more questions than it answered.

Shameka's phone buzzed, cutting through the tension. She looked at the screen. "It's my mom's lawyer. I wonder why he's calling so late," she said nervously and answered. "Hello?"

"Good evening, Ms. Shales. This is Darnell Patterson," the voice on the other end said, calm and steady.

"Is my mom okay?" she blurted out.

"She's fine," Patterson assured her. "I know it's late, but I knew you'd want to hear this information right away. I just heard from Detective Ridley. Your mother will be released tomorrow."

Shameka gasped as relief washed over her, tears streaming down her face as she clutched the phone.

Patterson gave her a moment before continuing. "The police have shifted their focus. The details are still unfolding, but you and your mother can return home. It's over."

Those words hung in the air.

"It's over," he repeated gently. "I'll send you details tomorrow about her release."

"Thank you," Shameka whispered, her voice breaking.

As she ended the call, KNote emerged from the bathroom, pale and unsteady. She caught the tail end of the conversation.

"It's over," she echoed, her tone bitter. "Over for *who*?"

She slowly walked to the nook and sank down, pulling the crochet blanket from the back of the chair over her legs and hung her head. "I guess that's it, then," she muttered, her voice hollow.

Hazel and Shameka turned toward her.

"What is?" Hazel asked, her head spinning with all the new information.

But KNote shook her head. "You don't have to pretend anymore," she said, not looking up. "Your mom is free. You don't need to keep helping me."

"KNote..." Shameka rushed over and knelt before her, shaking her head. "Yes, my mom is free. But we're not done here. We will figure out what happened to your mom. You're not alone in this."

Hazel added firmly, "We started this together, and we'll finish it together. Okay?"

KNote blinked, her eyes red and puffy. Slowly, she nodded, clutching the blanket tighter. "Really?"

"Of course." Shameka confirmed.

Hazel clapped her hands together, breaking the somber mood. "All right. We've got new information. We need to start fresh. What do we know? Let's lay it all out like a puzzle."

Shameka's face lit up with determination. Looking around she said, "We need a murder board!"

Hazel raised an eyebrow. "A what now?"

"A murder board," Shameka explained. "You know, like in detective shows? Timelines, suspects, motives—it helps organize everything."

KNote managed a faint smile. "Oh, I get it. Yeah, we have a whiteboard in the back. Will that do?"

"That'll do!" Shameka nodded enthusiastically.

"Okay, I'll get it." She disappeared again, leaving the two women alone.

Hazel turned to Shameka. "Thank you," Hazel said quietly.

"For what?"

"For sticking with this. For sticking with her."

Shameka shrugged. "We've all lost something in this mess. If I were in KNote's shoes, I'd hope someone would stick by me too. Plus, I want to see the monster responsible for this living nightmare put away."

KNote returned, pushing the board into the nook, a glimmer of determination in her eyes.

"It's time," she said, setting up the board. "Let's figure this out."

The three women leaned in, ready to unravel the tangled threads of a mystery that had consumed their lives.

Chapter 21: Later Saturday Night

Hazel and Shameka pushed the table with the leftover food out of the way, making room for the investigation. The cozy shop nook, usually a haven for crocheters, knitters and spinners, took on an entirely different energy—a makeshift war room. KNote wheeled in the whiteboard, setting it up in the center of the space, while Hazel grabbed dry erase markers in various colors from the cash desk.

The three women stood around the whiteboard, their expressions a mix of determination and uncertainty.

"Okay, now what? Where do we start?" KNote asked, breaking the silence.

Hazel tapped the marker against her chin, puzzling the question. "Let's start with the timeline. If we can map out when everything happened, maybe we'll spot something we missed—something that doesn't add up."

Shameka nodded and uncapped a marker. "This feels like something out of a true-crime podcast," she said with a nervous laugh, drawing a horizontal line across the board. "Except we're the ones living it."

Piece by piece, they began reconstructing the events, using the meticulous information Shameka had collected and what KNote had learned from the police.

"Okay, Thursday afternoon," KNote started, folding her arms tightly across her chest. "Hazel arrived at the shop around noon. Staff were busy rushing around with last-minute prep for the book signing. But everything seemed normal."

Shameka jotted this down.

"Then Hazel left," KNote said. "Around 5:00 p.m., guests started arriving for the event. I wasn't here, though.

"Then, how would you know what was happening if you weren't here?" Shameka asked, her brows furrowed.

"My mom called me just before Hazel got back, around 6:00 p.m.," KNote explained. "She always calls me about events at the shop when I can't be there to help. She mentioned how hectic it was. People were browsing yarn, chatting...nothing out of the norm. Everything seemed fine at the time."

"Okay," Shameka said, glancing over at Hazel. "What about when you got back?"

Hazel stepped forward, closer to the board. "I got back just before 6:00 p.m. The shop was buzzing—people shopping, chatting, and mingling around the food. Shanice greeted me and led me to the book signing area. I remember noticing a woman at the trunk show table grumbling about the yarn prices." She paused. "I later found out that was your mom, Shameka."

Shameka glanced at Hazel. She wrote down the note, her jaw working hard to school her warring emotions. "What happened next?"

"I gave my talk, took questions, and signed books. Everything seemed normal, but...now that I think about it, there was one thing." Hazel hesitated, then continued. "After Shanice introduced me, she was holding a glass of wine. She took a sip and muttered something about it tasting off—like it had gone bad. She didn't seem worried, though."

"Could the morphine have been in the wine?" KNote asked, her voice tight.

"Possibly," Shameka said, making a note on the board. "Or it could've been in her food. Either way, someone had to slip it to her."

"But who would have access to morphine?" Hazel asked. "It's a controlled substance. You don't just pick it up at the corner drugstore."

KNote pulled out her phone and searched the internet quickly. She read, "It says here on this website that morphine is used by cancer patients, hospice care—anyone dealing with severe pain. I've studied this in school. It can be addictive so it is highly monitored." She glanced up. "Who had access?"

"And whoever did this would need to be close enough to drug her food or drink, and then inject her later." Shameka added. "It has to be someone she trusted."

The group fell silent, the weight of the conversation settling over them.

"Let's go back to what the potential motives are," Hazel said, rubbing her temples where a headache started to form. "We've got blackmail and embezzlement on the table. Could it be one person doing both? Or are we dealing with two separate crimes?"

KNote added another note to the board. "Who would benefit from a blackmailing scheme? We should look into who's suddenly coming into more money."

"Jenika's driving around in a new Mustang," Hazel pointed out.

"That was from her mom's life insurance," KNote interjected. "She told us that when her mom passed away last year, she made Jenika promise to use part of the money for that car. It was something they both had wanted to take on a cross-country road trip, but she died before they could make it happen."

"Oh, that's so sad," Hazel said.

"So not her," Shameka said, crossing Jenika's name off their suspect list. "What about Jules? She's diabetic, so she knows how to handle needles."

"But that doesn't mean she has access to morphine," Hazel pointed out.

"True," KNote agreed, adding a question mark next to Jules's name. "But she's the store manager. How could she not know something fishy was going on with the books? We're still missing something. We should check her medicine bag to see if she has morphine in there."

Hazel's gaze lingered to the board. "Maybe...but would she carry it around with her every day? Was she planning on using it that day and she brought it in to use? Or does she have it on her person every day, and was waiting for the opportunity to put her plan in motion?"

No one spoke. The possibilities hung in the air.

This was not something Hazel had thought about. Was the murder premeditated or spur of the moment? That changed everything.

"And another thing," Hazel said, now on a roll. "It has to be Jules because she's the store manager, right? And she would have caught on to the discrepancies if it was someone else, making her the target."

"I've known Jules for years. I trust her," KNote stated.

"Yeah, and whoever did this, your mom trusted...at least enough to get close to her," Shameka stated matter-of-factly as she added the notes to the board.

"Wait..." Hazel said, flipping through Shameka's stack of papers. "There's something in one of the interviews Detective Ridley conducted. Here..." she scanned quickly. "Jenika said that Shanice and Jules argued that day. She said she didn't know what the argument was all about. But what if Shanice found out about the embezzlement and confronted her, and then Jules killed her to cover it all up?"

"That's a huge leap," KNote said softly. "They have been friends forever. Jules is like family."

"We have to consider every possibility," Hazel replied gently.

"I know. It's just hard to hear," KNote confessed. She puffed out a breath and said, "What else?"

"What about that photo we found in Shanice's safe?" Hazel asked after a moment. "The one of her holding a baby?"

KNote's face went pale. Avoiding their eyes, she said, "A few years ago, I found out I was adopted. When I asked my mom, she said she always wanted a daughter and didn't let not having a partner stop her. She's always made me feel loved, but..." Her voice cracked. "That baby in the photo? It looked so much like her. It makes me wonder...I've been thinking about it and staring at the photo a lot. Did she have a child before me? And if so, what happened to them?"

Shameka and Hazel exchanged looks before moving closer to KNote, placing comforting hands on her shoulders.

"She loved you," Hazel said softly. "That much is obvious. Anyone could see it. I saw it that day I met you and saw the two of you together. You and your mom had a bond that went well beyond blood."

"I know," KNote whispered. "But I can't stop wondering. I can't help it."

For a moment, they sat together in silence, drawing strength from one another.

KNote straightened, her resolve returning. She turned back to the board, her expression hardening. "I did ask Detective Ridley why they left my mom's office such a mess," KNote said. "He said that wasn't them."

She glanced at Hazel, then continued. "And because we cleaned it all up, he didn't see a point in coming out to dust for prints or anything."

"So someone ransacked your mom's office. They must have been searching for something." Shameka asked while making notes on the board. "Did they find it?"

"We need to keep digging. If we're going to figure this out, we need to think like the killer. Tomorrow, we'll start interviewing potential suspects," KNote said firmly. "And be careful. If they've killed once before, they'll do it again."

Hazel and Shameka nodded.

Hazel stared at the whiteboard, its surface crammed with notes, arrows, and scrawled questions. They had motives, opportunities, and a handful of suspects, but no solid leads.

"We seem to have more questions now than before we started," Hazel murmured to herself.

The mystery wasn't over. Not even close.

Later, as Hazel lay in bed, staring at the ceiling, her thoughts spiraled. She turned over in her head all that had unfolded with Shameka and KNote. Somewhere in this tangled web was a killer. And it was likely the name of someone they had on the murder board.

Chapter 22: Sunday Morning

H azel rose early, slipping into another pattern from her book, a cardigan with a colorwork yoke over light blue jeans. The outfit was comfortable yet polished, fitting for a day of subtle interrogation and public appearance. She was determined to be in the dining room for breakfast. She wanted to catch their main suspects, Jules and Jenika, before everyone headed to Yarn-monious for the day's retreat events.

At Yarn-monious, Hazel would be available to assist attendees in selecting sweater quantities of yarn, all while keeping up appearances and pretending that everything was fine. KNote would be welcoming and playing host to the retreat-goers with her usual charm, and Shameka would focus on her newly freed mother. With Verna no longer the prime suspect, Hazel doubted anyone would openly share what they knew with Shameka.

Guess that's it. Time to channel Miss Marple, Hazel thought grimly. And find the threads of truth and unravel this mess.

Settling into the corner seat in the bustling dining room, Hazel sipped cranberry juice, scanning the retreat attendees and regular hotel guests. Just the night before, this same corner had been a makeshift meeting spot for unraveling clues with Shameka and KNote. Hazel marveled at how quickly everything had changed. Was that really just last night?

Her foot tapped nervously under the table as she waited, unsure if Jenika or Jules would come in. Though local, they'd been joining the retreat attendees for breakfast every morning. She hoped today wouldn't be any exception.

Finally, Jenika strolled in, her bright smile lighting up the room. She wore a fitted black jumpsuit paired with an oversized knit cardigan draped effortlessly over her shoulders. The faint blond regrowth on her shaved head caught the overhead fluorescent lights. Hazel noticed something else, an energy about Jenika that seemed...different.

Hazel tracked Jenika's movement around the room as she navigated the breakfast stations, balancing an omelet, fruit, a waffle, and coffee on her tray. When their eyes met, Hazel waved her over.

"Hey," Jenika greeted, sliding into the seat across from her. "I don't usually see you here for breakfast."

"I know," Hazel admitted, ducking her head. "I'm usually too anxious about my class to eat. But since there are no classes today, I figured it was a good day to hangout and enjoy the atmosphere." She gestured at the bustling dining room, the air filled with the hum of chatter and the clinking of utensils.

"Yeah, I get it. It's a total vibe," Jenika said, digging into her omelet.

Silence settled over them, broken only by the sounds of breakfast around them. Hazel wrung her hands, unsure how to steer the conversation. Just dive in, she told herself.

"Um..." She cleared her throat. "Did you hear about Verna?" She said, carefully watching for a reaction.

Jenika looked up, her fork paused mid-air. "No. What about her?"

"They're letting her go. Something about not enough evidence." Hazel leaned forward. "Which means the police have to start over with suspects."

Jenika's expression tightened briefly before she resumed eating. "That's unfortunate. Everyone thought this nightmare was all over."

"I know." Hazel feigned nonchalance, sipping her juice. "But now it makes you wonder. If it wasn't Verna, then who else could it be?"

Jenika's glance flickered downward before she replied. "I have no idea."

Jenika was almost done with her breakfast but Hazel needed more information before she left...but what?

Hazel bit the inside of her cheek, considering her next move. "Um...Shanice wasn't married. Was she seeing anyone?" she asked, stumbling over each word.

Jenika froze, a fork-full of waffle hovering in the air halfway to her mouth. "No," she said sharply.

Hazel tilted her head, studying Jenika closely. "Why the hesitation?"

Jenika sighed, setting her fork down. "There's...there's just this ugly rumor going around that she was having an affair."

"An affair? With who?" Hazel pressed, raising a perfectly arched eyebrow to encourage her to continue.

"One of the retreat teachers." Jenika blew out a breath. She placed her elbows on the table and leaned in. Lowering her breath, she said, "A couple of weeks ago I had to come back to the shop after closing hours. I got all the way home and realized I'd forgotten my sweater sample I was working on for the shop. I drove back. I didn't have to use my key to get in because Shanice was still there, but she wasn't alone. As I entered through the front door, I saw someone leaving out the back. Shanice came out of her office looking...disheveled. Her sweater was buttoned wrong, like she'd rushed to do them up."

"Do you know who it was that was leaving?" Hazel pressed, leaning forward.

Jenika hesitated, glancing around the room before whispering. "Yeah, I do. It was Selene."

Hazel's stomach churned.

Jenika continued, her tone conspiratorial. "Getting in and out of the shop is easy if you know how. You go down the alley behind the shops and use the back door. It's always unlocked until the last person leaves and locks up."

Hazel's mind raced to piece together the implications. Could that be how the killer got in? If someone had entered after the book signing, after all the employees had left, they'd need to know about the back door. That narrowed down the list of suspects. It had to be someone with insider knowledge about the shop's operations.

Jenika pushed her plate away and stood. "I'll meet you in the lobby later to take you to Yarn-monious," she said before leaving the dining room.

Hazel remained seated at the table, her thoughts spinning. What did it all mean? Did the affair have anything to do with Shanice's murder? Hazel turned the conversation with Jenika around in her head. She was left with more questions than answers.

Pulling out her phone, she sent quick updates to KNote and Shameka:

Hazel: *Just spoke with Jenika.*

Shameka: *Be careful.*

Hazel: *Thanks, I will. Go take care of your mom.*

KNote: *We'll talk more when you get to the shop.*

Hazel set her phone done and sighed. Jenika had given her a crucial piece of the puzzle, but it only raised more questions.

Who could Selene have been protecting? Or implicating? And was the affair motive enough for murder?

Hazel drained the last of her cranberry juice, steeling herself for the day ahead. The truth was there, hidden, and she was determined to uncover it.

Chapter 23: Sunday Morning

Later that morning, Hazel sat at the hotel lobby, knitting needles clicking softly as she worked on the leg of her travel project—a pair of plain, cuff-down socks. The first sock had come off her needles the night before, and she'd cast on the second one right after breakfast. The ribbing was finished, and the meditative rhythm of plain stockinette stitching helped her focus amid the turmoil swirling in her mind.

A sharp ding signaled the elevator doors opening. Hazel glanced up just in time to spot Selene stepping out, surprisingly alone. For once, her usual entourage wasn't in tow.

Hazel saw an opportunity she couldn't afford to miss. Her pulse quickened. This was the moment. She tucked her knitting into her bag, stood, and intercepted Selene with a steady but quiet urgency.

"Selene, do you have a second?" Hazel asked, her voice steady despite her nerves.

Selene paused, arching one perfect brow, her lips already curling into a dismissive 'no'. But Hazel pressed on, she wasn't going to back down.

"It's important," Hazel said, her voice low but firm. "It's about your *relationship* with Shanice," she added, emphasizing the word, relationship.

Selene froze mid-step. Her perfectly polished mask cracking just slightly, replaced by a flicker of fear and anger. Her eyes darted around the lobby and without a word, she grabbed Hazel's elbow and dragged her into a quiet corner.

"What do you want?" Selene hissed, her tone sharp as glass. "To expose me? Ruin me? Is this revenge for that email years ago?"

"What? No!" Hazel blinked, startled. "This isn't about that."

Selene's eyes narrowed, suspicion blazing. "Then why bring it up? What's your angle?"

Hazel exhaled slowly to steady herself. "Your relationship with Shanice isn't my concern. I just need to know—did it have *anything* to do with her murder?"

Selene recoiled as if Hazel had slapped her. "Her...*murder*? Are you accusing me?"

"No!" Hazel rushed to clarify, raising her hands in placation. "I just—"

"Stop." Selene's voice wavered, then dropped to a whisper, hoarse with emotion. "I love..." She swallowed hard, her voice breaking. "I loved her," she admitted.

Hazel said nothing, patiently waiting for Selene to continue.

After a moment, Selene glanced around again, her usual confidence crumbling. "I loved her," she repeated, softer this time, as though testing the words on her tongue. Her words came out haltingly, raw. Her throat bobbed as she swallowed. "But she ended it. Someone saw us, and she didn't want to risk...everything."

"Risk what?" Hazel asked gently.

Selene's eyes turned glassy. "My career. My *life*. If this gets out, I'll lose *everything*. My family. My book deals. My partnerships, everything I've built on my squeaky-clean image. But I didn't kill her. I *couldn't*."

Hazel stayed firm, though the raw vulnerability in Selene's voice tugged at her. "You know people think Verna did it. But what if they're wrong? What if—"

Selene's gaze snapped to Hazel's, sharp and full of fire. "What part of 'I *loved* her' don't you understand?" Her voice cracked on the last word. "Love doesn't make you a killer. Someone breaking up with you that you don't agree with doesn't make you a killer."

"Jenika mentioned that the breakup was messy and loud." Hazel pressed, her voice steady but probing.

Selene's lips pressed into a thin line. "I didn't do anything wrong. Yes, I was upset. Of course, I was upset," she repeated, her voice firm and direct. "Who wouldn't be? That's normal."

"Could someone have known about your relationship and been blackmailing you and Shanice to keep it quiet?" Hazel asked, her tone deliberate. "Were *you* blackmailing Shanice?"

"What? No! That's absurd." Selene shot back, incredulous.

Hazel didn't flinch.

"Why would I do that?" Selene demanded.

"To keep your relationship a secret. Maybe Shanice threatened to tell. Maybe you were angry. You could've snuck in through the back door undetected. You've done it many times before." Hazel guessed, her words coming out sharper than she intended.

Seeing Selene's reaction, she knew she'd hit the nail on the head.

Selene's eyes flashed, but she held her ground. "Why would I do that? I told you, I didn't kill her. It was a breakup, that's all! You're not going to give up, are you?" She exhales sharply, crossing her arms. "Fine. I'll tell you because I *didn't* kill her. After your book signing, I went to her office to try to convince her to take me back. I promised we'd be more discreet this time."

"And?" Hazel asked, leaning in slightly.

"She said no," Selene said, her voice softening, the hurt cutting through her usual poise. "She said my future was too important to her."

"What time was that?" Hazel asked.

"Around 9 p.m. I was there for less than fifteen minutes," Selene replied.

"Did you see anyone else there?"

"No," Selene's jaw tightened, her polished mask slipping further. "I often used the back door. At that time of night, the shops are closed, and the street is empty. I didn't see anyone and I don't know if anyone saw me. I was upset and crying all the way back to my car in the Municipal Parking Lot."

"Can anyone corroborate your version of events?"

Selene shook her head. "No."

Hazel tilted her head and watched Selene carefully. "How did Shanice seem when you were with her?"

Selene hesitated, her brows knitted together. "Tired. She kept yawning. She said it had been a long day."

Hazel softened her tone, but she pushed on, her gaze never wavering. "Do you know who *would* have wanted to hurt her?"

Selene let out a sharp breath, her shoulders sagged slightly. For a moment, her vulnerability was laid bare, a mixture of grief and helplessness. Hazel saw a real person under the facade.

"No," Selene murmured, her voice barely a whisper. "I don't know. Maybe someone she crossed professionally. Or..." She shook her head, as if dismissing a thought she couldn't bear to voice.

Hazel caught the hesitation. "Or what?"

"Maybe they've got the right person in custody. Maybe it *is* Verna. She doesn't have an alibi, does she? She can't prove she wasn't there."

Hazel's brow furrowed. "How do you know she doesn't have an alibi?" she asked, her voice careful. Did Selene know more than she was saying?

"It's obvious," Selene snapped, a flicker of defensiveness in her eyes. "If she had one, the police wouldn't still have her in custody." Her voice cracked, but she pressed on. "Look, I don't know what happened. But it wasn't me. I loved her. That's all I know. And now..." her voice faltered. "Now, she's gone."

The two women stared at each other. Hazel studied her, the silence between them heavy with unanswered questions. A single tear broke free, streaking down Selene's cheek before she wiped it away with a quick and furious swipe.

Then, as quickly as it had slipped, her mask slid back into place. Selene straightened, lifted her chin and squared her shoulders. "I have nothing else to say. Especially to you," she declared, her tone turned icy.

Without waiting for a response, Selene turned and strode away, her heels clicking sharply against the polished floor, her head held high, daring anyone to question her.

Hazel stood rooted to the spot, watching her retreat, conflicted and uneasy. The vulnerability she'd glimpsed still gnawed at her, leaving her unsettled. Love doesn't make you a killer, she thought.

Hazel wanted to believe it. She'd cling to the hope. But something didn't sit right.

Chapter 24: Sunday Morning

"There you are," Jenika called out, emerging from a nearby conference room with a large tote bag slung over her shoulder. Her bright tone didn't quite mask the exhaustion shadowing her eyes. "Ready to head over to Yarn-monious?"

"Ready," Hazel replied, forcing a smile that didn't reach her eyes. It felt tight and brittle, far from convincing.

The drive to the yarn shop was steeped in silence. Hazel stared out the window, the scenery blurring into a streak of color as her mind spiraled through the tangled threads of clues and suspicions. Her mental murder board was a jumbled chaos: suspects pinned, motives scrawled, connections blurred. Every new thought only tightened the knot in her stomach.

Jenika's hands gripped the steering wheel, her knuckles pale against the leather. She seemed lost in her own thoughts, her usually chatty demeanor subdued. She didn't attempt to break the quiet with small talk, and Hazel didn't mind. It wasn't an awkward silence, it was heavier than that. Dense. Foreboding. Like the air before a storm.

When they finally pulled up to the shop, Jenika slowed to a stop at the curb. "I'll go park in the Municipal lot and meet you inside," she said, her tone neutral, her gaze flicking briefly toward Hazel.

Hazel nodded, her hand lingering on the door handle for a moment too long. "Thanks," she said before stepping out.

On the sidewalk, a makeshift shrine honoring Shanice stood as a somber reminder of the loss that still rippled through the community. Flickering candles surrounded bouquets of flowers, handwritten notes, and photos of Shanice' warm, radiant smile. A small cluster of people stood nearby, heads bowed in quiet reverence. Hazel slowed her steps as she passed, her chest tightening, before she pushed open the shop door.

The familiar cheerful tinkle of the bell above the entrance felt jarring, almost disrespectful against the somber scene outside. Inside, the shop buzzed with activity. Knitters and crocheters chatting animatedly as they browsed shelves and bins of yarn. The hum of conversation heightened Hazel's anxiety. Two charter buses full of retreat attendees were due to arrive soon, and the thought of the influx made her stomach knot.

At the cash desk, KNote stood talking with Jules. She wore her mom's oversized cardigan over a flowing floor-length dress and cowboy boots. Hazel made a beeline for them.

"Good morning, KNote. Jules," Hazel greeted, her voice steady despite the unease bubbling inside her.

"Good morning," they chorused.

Jules adjusted the strap of her messenger bag, which rested on the counter, its flap slightly ajar. Hazel's gaze caught on the familiar pouch inside—the one Jules carried to the bathroom the other day. Her curiosity flared. Could it hold something incriminating?

"Excuse me," Jules said abruptly, stepping away. "Could you watch the desk? I'll be back shortly. Suki and Jenika will be here soon."

The moment Jules disappeared, Hazel leaned in and whispered to KNote, "Keep an eye out. I need to check something."

Heart pounding, Hazel opened the pouch. Syringes, insulin, a glucose meter, and bottles of pills, including an antidepressant, filled the space. It all looked innocent enough until her eyes landed on the needle tips. She pulled out the tiny piece of plastic she'd found in the trashed office and compared it. A perfect match.

Her breath hitched. This is what the killer had been searching for.

The bathroom door creaked open. Hazel scrambled to replace everything and closed the pouch just as Jules returned.

"All set," Jules said, reclaiming her spot behind the desk.

Hazel turned to KNote, her mind racing. "We need to talk," she murmured.

They retreated to the office, closing the door behind them. Hazel explained her discovery.

"It matches the needle cover," she said, holding up the plastic piece. "The killer must have dropped it that night."

"Do you think Jules is the killer?" KNote asked, her voice tight with tension.

"I don't know," Hazel admitted, exhaling sharply.

"Okay, let's put a pin in that. Tell me, what else happened at the hotel?" KNote asked.

Hazel shared everything she'd learned from Selene.

KNote's expression crumbled. "Mom never told me she was involved with anyone. I feel like I didn't really know her at all. People keep showing up to give condolences and sharing stories about her. They have all these memories with her, and I don't even know what they are talking about."

Hazel placed a comforting hand on her shoulder. "I think there are parts of our parents' lives we'll never know because they were whole people before us. When my mom died, I had people tell stories about her I had never heard of. It was hard to hear. I felt excluded. But over the years, I've come to realize that my mom was a person with a life, dreams and desires before she was my mom. And so was yours. Don't let what you didn't know about her overshadow the memories you do have."

KNote nodded, wiping her eyes. "Thanks, Hazel." She took a deep breath, physically shaking herself to refocus on the mission—figure out who killed her mom. "So, what now? Does this mean we have another suspect to add to the list...Selene?"

Hazel hesitated. "I don't know. I believed her when she said she loved your mom. I don't think she hurt her."

"But if not her, then who?" KNote groaned, frustration clear in her voice. "We're back to square one. I don't know how much more of this I can take."

They looked at each other. Neither ready to give up, but not knowing where to go next.

The shop buzzed as the first busload of retreat attendees arrived. Any further investigation would have to wait. KNote picked up a partially completed crochet corner-to-corner project her mom had been working on—a teal triangle with a heart forming in the center. She was determined to finish it to honor her mom.

With shoulders squared and head held high, KNote clutched the crochet piece tightly and stepped out to greet the crowd. Hazel followed closely behind, ready to lend a supporting hand if needed.

As the shop filled with cheerful voices, Hazel couldn't shake the feeling that the real killer was among them, maybe here right now, watching and waiting.

The killer is still out here.

Chapter 25: Sunday Afternoon

The shop buzzed with energy, the retreat attendees mingling among displays of vibrant yarns, their laughter and chatter blending with the soft music of Shanice's album playing in the background.

Melinda entered the shop, her eyes lit up when she spotted Hazel.

"Hazel!" Melinda waved enthusiastically, holding up a neatly blocked swatch. Hazel returned the gesture with a bright smile, energized by the familiar comfort of yarn and community. This was her zone, her happy place.

"This looks fantastic," Hazel said, leaning in to examine the swatch. Her fingers brushed over the stitches with practiced care. "Let's figure out how much yarn you'll need for your sweater."

Flipping through her book and referencing lessons from class, Hazel guided Melinda through the process of selecting the perfect yarn for her project and calculating how much yarn she'll need. Soon, a small crowd formed, attendees holding swatches and questions in hand. Hazel moved seamlessly from one to the next, offering tips, modifications, and encouragement to build confidence in their choices.

As the day wore on, the shop slowly emptied. The last of the attendees and teachers filed onto the chartered bus, their purchases clutched tightly. Hazel was spent, her feet aching and her voice hoarse. Yet, a deep sense of satisfaction settled over her. She sank into the cozy nook, and pulled out her travel sock project, letting the soothing rhythm of the stitches calm her mind.

Around her, the shop's buzz softened to a quiet hum with the last flurry of activity. KNote was expertly assisting a few lingering shoppers, her voice warm and patient. Behind the cash desk, Jules rang up final purchases with precision, her movements brisk but efficient. Meanwhile, Jenika and Suki moved quietly through the shop, tidying displays and restocking shelves.

Hazel let her eyes wander before returning to her knitting, her thoughts turning inward. The murder board she'd assembled with KNote and Shameka flashed in her mind, a tangled web of clues and connections that felt as chaotic as her own hurried notes.

She ran through the list of evidence they'd compiled, mentally sorting through what they knew and what remained elusive. The glaring gaps mocked her, each one representing a question unanswered, a detail overlooked.

What was still missing? And who was working so hard to keep it hidden?

Hazel's gaze drifted around the shop where the faint hum of conversation was giving way to the quieter sounds of closing time. Somewhere out there, the truth was waiting, shrouded in half-truths and secrets. She tightened her grip on her knitting needles, determination rising within her.

The final pieces were out there, and she was getting closer.

The door swung open with a rush of icy air, breaking Hazel's reverie. Shameka entered, pausing to glance around as she unwrapped her scarf. Her eyes scanned the room until they landed on KNote, who was deep in conversation with a customer. Shameka raised a hand in greeting, and KNote, mid-sentence, waved back absently.

Scanning the room again, Shameka's gaze settled on Hazel. A flicker of urgency crossed her face as she headed directly to her.

Sliding into the seat beside her, Shameka leaned in, practically bouncing with contained energy. "Hey, I've got news," she said, her voice low but insistent. "But let's wait for KNote."

Hazel studied Shameka's expression, a mix of excitement and worry. "How's your mom?"

Shameka had emailed earlier that she would be picking up her mom from the holding station and bringing her home. But she didn't mention that she'd be at Yarn-monious today. What could be so important for her to come to the shop instead of staying with her mom?

Shameka exhaled deeply, her shoulders slumping. "She's recovering...slowly," she admitted. "Even though she was only in there for a short time, she's having nightmares about being arrested again. She's terrified, Hazel. We have to figure out who killed Shanice. It's the only way she'll ever feel free."

Hazel reached out, giving Shameka's hand a comforting pat.

"Besides, she has her two best friends over—Aunties Ava and Jazmyn," Shameka added with a wistful smile. "They're not really my aunts, but I've known them my whole life. They've been Mom's best friends since college." She paused, her gaze distant as if replaying a cherished memory. A glimmer of amusement lit her eyes. "They were in the kitchen drinking tea—though I'm pretty sure it had something stronger than milk," she added in a conspiratorial whisper. Her smile grew, warmth radiating from her. "I think she's going to be okay."

Hazel chuckled, the brief levity easing some of the tension. "It sounds like she has good people around her."

Moments later, KNote rushed over, her movements sharp and hurried. She dropped into the chair, breathless. "What's going on?" she asked, her voice taut with urgency, her chest rising and falling as she tried to catch her breath.

Shameka turned to KNote, her expression soft but tinged with apprehension. "Have you heard from Detective Ridley? Or your mom's attorney?"

KNote shook her head, frustration flickering in her eyes like a storm. "No," she said, her voice tight. "I don't have my phone on me. It's been chaotic here all day. Between all the shoppers and people seeing that the shop has re-opened and popping in to pay their condolences, I haven't had a second to breathe, let alone think." She glanced around the room, the stress of the day was obvious on her face. "Wait, I'll grab my phone," she said and gestured toward the office at the back of the shop.

She began to rise, but Shameka reached out, her hand warm and firm on KNote's arm, stopping her in her tracks. "Stay. I have to tell you something," Shameka said, her voice low, almost urgent.

KNote froze, her sharp gaze darting between Shameka and Hazel. "What is it? What's going on?" she asked, her tone threading between worry and demand.

Shameka hesitated, clasping and unclasping her hands in her lap, her nerves betraying her even as she tried to remain composed. She inhaled deeply, as if bracing herself for impact. "When I was at the police station earlier picking up my mom..." She paused, searching for the right words. "I overheard something you need to know."

KNote leaned forward, her body taut with tension. "Just tell me," she said, her voice cracking slightly under the weight of anticipation.

Shameka's gaze met KNote's, her own filled with a mix of sympathy and urgency. "Okay, I'm just gonna say it," she whispered. "They've found adoption records for a baby Shanice gave up years ago. A baby girl." She glanced down for a moment before continuing. "It must have been when she was in the girl group."

Her words hung in the air, heavy and charged, as KNote's face shifted from shock, confusion, and something deeper rippling across her features.

KNote shot to her feet, her movements jittery with barely contained energy. She paced the small space like a caged animal, her steps erratic and forceful. The tension in the air thickened as Hazel and Shameka watched her with concern. Without warning, KNote strode toward the office, her hands balled into fists.

Hazel and Shameka exchanged a glance before following her to the office and closed the door behind them.

"Who is she?" KNote asked sharply, her words tumbling out in rapid succession.

"They don't know yet," Shameka said softly, her voice carrying the weight of the unknown. "That's all I heard at the station."

KNote exhaled sharply, running a hand over her face, her frustration palpable. "She'd be older than I am. I have so many questions. Did she know who my mom was and where she was?" KNote asked half to herself, desperate to understand what was going on.

"What does it mean, though? Could she have something to do with Shanice's death?" Hazel asked, her voice quieter but no less urgent.

Shameka shook her head slowly. "It's impossible to know. She might be a person of interest, but there's no clear connection. How would she even fit into the motives or have access to Shanice?"

KNote pressed her hands against the edge of the desk as she tried to steady herself. Hazel stepped closer, her tone gentle but firm. "KNote, how are you holding up? I know you've suspected that your mom might've had a child before you, but hearing it confirmed like this...it's a lot."

For a moment, KNote looked like she might crumble under the weight of it all. Her lips parted as if to speak, but a knock at the door cut her short. She closed her eyes, drawing in a shaky breath to regain her composure. "Come in," she said, her tone clipped but controlled.

The door opened slightly, and Jules peeked her head inside, her demeanor calm but purposeful. "Sorry to interrupt," she said, glancing around between the three women with suspicion. "The last customers just left, and the shop is cleaned up. We're heading out," she said, gesturing toward the rest of the staff.

Jules' gaze shifted to settle on Hazel. "Jenika's ready to take you back to the hotel if you're ready."

"Of course. I'll be right there. Thank you, Jules," Hazel nodded, offering a quick smile.

As the door clicked shut behind Jules, Hazel turned back to KNote, her expression softening. "I know this is a lot. And I know you want answers," she said gently. "But it's been a long day. Go home, get some rest. We'll figure this out together, I promise."

KNote opened her mouth to protest, her frustration and exhaustion evident, but Hazel stepped forward and wrapped her in a firm, grounding hug. For a moment, KNote remained rigid, before exhaling deeply. Her shoulders sagged, the tension draining from her body as she allowed herself to lean into the embrace.

When Hazel pulled back, she turned to Shameka and offered a brief but heartfelt hug.

"I'll text you when I get to the hotel," she assured them.

Gathering her bag and knitting project from the nook, Hazel made her way toward the front of the shop. Outside, the rain drummed against the windows, icy and unrelenting. Jenika had gone ahead to retrieve the car from the Municipal Lot and promised to meet Hazel out front.

Stepping into the biting cold, Hazel winced as the rain stung her cheeks, the wind carrying a sharp chill that seeped through her scarf. Jenika pulled up, and Hazel quickly climbed into the car, grateful for the warmth inside.

Her heart felt heavy with unanswered questions and the unspoken pain in her friends' eyes. The new information confirming the baby Shanice put up for adoption all those years again must mean something. But what? How does it fit?

Chapter 26: Sunday Evening

Rain poured down in icy sheets, soaking into the earth and chilling everything to the bone. Jenika drove cautiously, the headlights cutting through the thick darkness of early evening. The rhythmic thrum of raindrops against the windshield and steady swish of the wiper blades filled the car.

Hazel stared out the window, her mind drifting. The storm mirrored her thoughts—unsettled and murky. Shameka's news about the baby Shanice put up for adoption left them with more questions. How does it fit in? Something niggled at the back of Hazel's mind, but she couldn't hold on to it. Every time she reached for it, the thought slipped away. When she got back to her hotel, she'd call KNote and Shameka and do some more sleuthing. Maybe together, they could unravel another thread.

At a stoplight, Jenika glanced into the backseat and frowned. "Shoot," she muttered. "I promised Selene I'd bring some yarn for her new collaboration with the shop, but I must've left the bag at home. Do you mind if we swing by my place to grab it?"

Hazel blinked out of her musing. "Sure," she replied absently, her gaze returning to the rain-slick streets.

As the car moved forward again, Hazel's mind wandered back to the investigation. Why had Jules argued with Shanice? Had Shanice caught Jules in the act and threatened to expose her? But Jules didn't seem sharp enough to orchestrate the complex pricing scam and embezzlement. Or at least, not alone. Was she a pawn, helping or covering for someone else? And if so, whose pawn?

"Wait—what did you just say?" Jenika asked, a note of curiosity in her voice.

Hazel stiffened, realizing she'd voiced her thoughts aloud. "Oh, nothing," she said quickly. "Just thinking."

"Thinking about what?" Jenika pressed, glancing over at Hazel before focusing back on the road.

Shifting uncomfortably in her seat, Hazel hesitated. "Just...wondering when I'll get to go home. The police are keeping some of us in town because of Shanice's murder."

"I'm sorry you're stuck here," Jenika said softly, her concern evident.

"Yeah, thanks," Hazel replied, her voice thin, her thoughts still miles away.

Jenika's tone shifted, becoming more casual but laced with intrigue. "I overheard you and KNote talking about Shanice's murder. Sounded like you two are playing detectives. Do you have any suspects yet?"

Hazel froze, her pulse quickening. "What?" she asked, caught off guard. Her head spun. She felt dizzy.

"Jules, maybe?" Jenika continued smoothly, as if Hazel hadn't spoken. "I heard she was arguing with Shanice the day she died. Did you know that?" Jenika didn't wait for an answer. "But, honestly, it probably wasn't her." Her words rolled out, calm and unhurried, as though they were discussing the weather.

Hazel turned to study Jenika. Why is she telling me this?

The car rolled to a stop in the driveway of a small, run-down bungalow. The headlights sliced through the rain, illuminating a house cloaked in shadows. Not a single light was on inside or out, leaving the place in eerie stillness. The overgrown lawn was hidden beneath a soggy carpet of autumn leaves, and weeds choked what remained of the flower beds.

Jenika pulled the car into park with a sharp jerk. The wipers squeaked against the glass in a losing battle against the downpour. She glanced over at Hazel, flashing a quick, almost forced smile. "Come on in," she said, her voice light but clipped.

She grabbed her purse and darted out, her shoes splashing through puddles on the cracked driveway. Weeds clawed their way up through the broken asphalt.

Hazel hesitated, her fingers clutching the edge of her seat. The house loomed ahead, its peeling paint glistening in the rain, shutters hanging askew. A single streetlight cast jittery shadows as Jenika climbed the steps, shielding herself with her bag.

Hazel climbed out reluctantly and followed, feeling uneasy. Jenika fumbled with the lock, finally shoving the door open.

Inside, the air was stale, like the windows hadn't been opened in years. The decor was outdated, faded carpeting and furniture from a bygone era, but everything was meticulously clean.

"Make yourself at home," Jenika said over her shoulder as she turned on a single lamp and disappeared down a dark hallway.

Hazel pulled out her phone and sent a quick message to Shameka and KNote. She didn't know how far she was from the hotel or how long it would be before she got back. She lingered in the living room, but her curiosity got the better of her. She wandered toward a room with the door slightly ajar. Pushing it open, she froze.

The room resembled a hospital ward. A high medical bed took up most of the space, flanked by an IV stand and a nightstand crowded with medicine bottles. The air smelled faintly of antiseptic. Hazel stepped inside, her eyes drawn to the labels on the bottles.

One name jumped out at her: *Robynn Stevenson*.

Her gaze fell on another bottle, this one labeled: *DIAMORPHINE*.

Framed photographs lined the walls and nightstand. Most were of Jenika, smiling alongside a striking woman with dark skin, cropped hair, and piercing eyes. Hazel's attention caught on a particular photo near the bed, a gold-framed image embossed with the word *LYRIX*.

Her breath hitched. It was the same photo that had been in Shanice's safe.

Hazel snapped a few photos and quickly shot them off to KNote and Shameka.

"What are you doing in here?"

Jenika's voice snapped through the air, sharp and furious.

Hazel spun, dropping her phone. She quickly picked up it up, her hands trembling. Jenika stormed into the room, her expression thunderous. She grabbed Hazel by the arm and shoved her toward the door.

"This room is private! Get out!" Jenika's voice cracked with anger, her composure shattering.

"I'm sorry," Hazel stammered, her heart pounding.

But Jenika wasn't listening. Her anger spilled over, her words tumbling out in a bitter rant. "Nosy people sticking their noses where they don't belong...always getting what they deserve."

The air between them crackled with tension as Hazel backed out of the room, her mind racing. Her instincts screamed that she'd just stumbled onto something critical.

Hazel knew she was in trouble.

Chapter 27: Sunday Evening

Hazel stumbled backward, her legs trembling beneath her. Her heart thundered in her chest, and her breath came in uneven gasps. The living room loomed around her, dimly lit by a single lamp casting long shadows against the walls. She collapsed onto an old couch, the cushions sagging under her weight. Her hand brushed against mismatched crochet blankets draped over it, their soft texture a cruel contrast to the tension crackling in the room.

Her gaze darted around the room, taking in the scattered family photos. Jenika's face smiled back at her from every angle: school pictures, vacations, moments frozen in time. But it was the images of her mother, Robynn, that held Hazel's attention.

In early photos, Robynn's beauty radiated: glowing brown skin, a dazzling smile, dark eyes full of life, and braids piled high on top of her head like a crown. But as Hazel's eyes traveled across the timeline of images, she saw the vitality fade. The braids gave way to headscarves, the glow dimmed, and the woman in the later photos was gaunt and hollow-eyed, a shadow of the vibrant person she once was. The toll of cancer was devastatingly evident.

"I know what you've been up to." Jenika's voice cut through the stillness, sharp and accusing.

Hazel's head snapped up. Jenika stood by the doorway, her figure half-shadowed, her eyes burning with anger, her lips curled in a snarl.

"You and your little friends," Jenika spat, stepping into the room. "KNote and Shameka playing detectives. I saw you earlier. Searching through Jules's bag. You thought no one noticed, but I did. I was outside, waiting for the first busload of retreat attendees to arrive. I glanced in and saw you holding up her needle, putting it all together."

Hazel froze, her mind racing for a response. Her throat felt dry, her palms clammy. The room seemed to close around her.

Hazel couldn't risk saying the wrong thing. Her eyes flicked to the photos on the wall, searching for a distraction.

"That was your mom?" she asked softly, pointing to one of the earlier pictures. Her voice wavered, but she pressed on. "She was very beautiful."

Jenika's face softened momentarily, a flicker of grief breaking through her anger. "Yes," she whispered, her voice cracking. "She was."

For a brief moment, her hardened demeanor softened. But then, just as quickly, the rage returned.

"She didn't deserve to die," Jenika hissed, her tone icy and sharp.

Hazel shifted slightly, instinct urging her to stand, to find a way out. But Jenika's eyes pinned her in place, as chilling as the threat in her tone.

"Make one more move and you'll be sorry," Jenika warned, and reached into her pocket.

Hazel's stomach dropped when she saw the glint of metal. She was already sorry for getting involved.

Jenika pulled out a syringe, the plastic cap falling to the floor as she flicked it off with her thumb. She pointed it at Hazel, her hand steady, her gaze unyielding.

"She'd still be here if Shanice had helped," Jenika spat, her voice trembling with barely restrained rage.

Hazel's stomach clenched, her pulse pounding in her ears. She forced herself to stay calm, to keep her voice steady. "What do you mean?" she asked, her tone measured, careful. Keeping her talking.

Jenika sank into an armchair across from Hazel, her movements slow and deliberate, her gaze fixed. She leaned forward, her elbows resting on her knees, the syringe still clutched in her hand.

"My mom told me I was adopted when she got sick," Jenika began, her tone bitter yet tinged with pain. "And near the end, she told me the truth about who my birth mother was. Wanna guess?" she paused. Without waiting for an answer, she blurted out, "Shanice. Yes, *the* famous Shanice," a hollow laugh, devoid of humor escaped her lips.

Hazel sat, helpless. She stayed silent, letting Jenika continue.

"She gave me away," Jenika said, her voice cracking. "Her precious pop star life was more important."

Jenika's eyes filled with tears, and she blinked them away.

"The beloved pop star turned yarn shop owner. Everyone thought she was so perfect...such a nice lady. But when I needed her, when my mom needed her, she refused to help."

"What happened?"

"I reached out to her," she paused, her lips pressing into a thin line as if the name itself tasted foul. "I sent her a picture of me as a baby, her holding me. Signed the letter with the name she gave me: Lyrix," she continued, her voice breaking. "I begged her for help, for money to get my mom the care insurance wouldn't cover. I was desperate. And you know what she said?"

Hazel swallowed hard, her voice barely a whisper. "What did she say?"

"She said no," Jenika snarled, her grip on the syringe tightened. "She could've helped but she refused. She had the money. My mom *died* because of her selfishness. And now I have no one. I'm all alone."

Jenika stared at a photo of her mom. Her voice dropped, cold and hollow. "I hated her for that. *She* deserved to die. Not my mom."

The room fell into a suffocating silence, the weight of Jenika's confession pressing down on Hazel like a lead blanket. Her mind raced, searching for a way out, a way to de-escalate the situation. The syringe gleamed under the dim light, a stark reminder of the danger just a few feet away.

"She took everything away from me," Jenika muttered, her face taking on a faraway look as if remembering a moment.

Hazel glances toward the front door, calculating the distance, the odds.

"Did you know I was studying to become a pharmacist?" Jenika continued, her voice almost conversational. "It was always a dream. I was almost through my studies. And then my mom got sick and everything changed. I had to drop out to help take care of her. It was okay in the beginning. There were nurses coming in."

A small smile crept across Jenika's face. In a flash it was gone, replaced with anger. "But as she got sicker and insurance kept denying her claims, I had to take on more and more of the responsibilities. It was okay though. She was my mom and I'd do anything for her," she glanced at a photo on the side table of Robynn in her younger and healthier years.

"Between taking care of mom and what I'd learned in school, it was easy. Did you know that you're supposed to dispose of all leftover medications when a person dies?" A grim look came over her face. "I kept them. I knew they'd come in handy."

"A few months went by, and I mourned my mom." Jenika's expression hardened, her voice sharpening. "And then one day, a plan clicked. I would end her and make her suffer like my mom suffered. I applied for and got a job at Yarn-monious under the name my mom gave me, not the one *that* woman gave me," she spat out, her words menacing. The syringe gripped tightly in her hand.

"You embezzled from the shop, didn't you?" Hazel asked as she tried to steer the conversation away from the syringe.

Jenika let out a bitter laugh. "Of course I did. It was so easy," she said, her voice laced with venom. "I wanted to take everything from Shanice, just like she took everything from me. I wanted her to pay, but it wasn't enough. At first, she turned a blind eye to the QR code scheme. But I demanded more. Weekly payments. And she gave in," Jenika's faced twisted cruelly.

"She had no problem coming up with the money to pay me off. She thought she was buying my silence."

"What changed?" Hazel asked cautiously, her mind racing to piece the puzzle together.

"Jules," Jenika said, her eyes narrowing. "She started poking around the shop's finances and asking questions. And Shanice? She finally decided she'd had enough."

Jenika let out a hollow laugh, her bitterness and disdain cutting through the air like a blade.

"The night before the book signing, Shanice threatened to turn me in. Can you believe that? She was willing to turn her own flesh and blood over to the police." She shook her head, her voice dropping to a chilling whisper. "We couldn't have that, now, could we? I wasn't done enacting my revenge."

Jenika looked down at the syringe, her fingers rolling it in her hand absentmindedly. Her voice softened, almost as if she was speaking to herself. "Everyone thought she was an angel," she muttered. "Every day, I had to listen to that stupid album on repeat. People think Eleven-Eleven is so deep and thoughtful and mystical. But it wasn't. Eleven-Eleven is my birthday." She shoved her wrist forward, revealing the inked numbers etched into her skin: *11:11*.

"She wrote a song about *me* and made millions. Millions she couldn't bother to use to save my mother." Her voice cracked, but her rage flared brighter. "She deserved what she got. And if I could have made her suffer more, I would have."

Hazel stared at Jenika, her heart aching at the depth of the woman's pain but chilled by her words.

Jenika leaned closer, her gaze locked on Hazel. "I took everything from her," she said, laughing maniacally. "And now you, sticking your nose where it doesn't belong. I've watched you. You walk around all high and mighty with your I-mind-my-own-business attitude. But no. You let KNote and Shameka drag you into this mess. What do y'all think this was? A PBS special of *Miss Marple*? You should've stayed out of it, Hazel."

Chapter 28: Sunday Evening

The weight of Jenika's words hung heavy in the air, each word pressing down on Hazel like a physical force. Her heart ached for Jenika. Her mother's illness, the burden of caregiving, the bitterness of being denied help when it was within reach, the pain of losing her mother. But Hazel couldn't let that empathy cloud her focus. She had to survive.

"You don't have to do this," Hazel pleaded, forcing her voice to remain steady despite the panic threatening to consume her. Her eyes darted to the syringe in Jenika's hand, then back to her face.

Jenika's expression hardened, her movement sharp as she stood abruptly. The syringe caught in the dim light, its gleaming surface an ominous threat. "Yes, I do," she snapped, her voice cold and unyielding. "You know too much."

Hazel's mind raced, grasping for any lifeline. "But if you kill me, they'll know it was you," she offered. "KNote and Shameka know I came here with you. They'll come looking for me."

Jenika hesitated, a flicker of doubt crossing her face. "They'll think something happened after I dropped you off at the hotel," she countered, though her voice lacked its earlier conviction.

"I texted them before we came here," she said, her voice shaky. "Told them I was running late because we were stopping by your house first. They'll call Detective Ridley if they don't hear from me."

Jenika's lips curved into a sneer. "That bumbling detective?" she scoffed. "He couldn't put two-and-two together to make four if you handed him the calculator. All he cares about is closing the case, and he already did, with Verna. Case closed."

Hazel shook her head, her tone calm but cutting. "You haven't heard, have you? Verna's been released. Verna is home. The case is still open. That's what Shameka came to the shop to tell us."

The words landed like a slap. Jenika's face contorted with rage and frustration. "Why couldn't you just mind your own business and leave it alone?" she screamed, her voice cracking under the weight of her fury.

Hazel flinched but kept her voice calm. "Please, Jenika. You don't have to do this," she begged, the blood pumped in her ears so loud she could hardly hear.

"Yes, I do. You know too much."

"Please let me go," Hazel whispered. "I promise I won't—"

"What," Jenika interrupted her with a laugh, "tell anyone? You won't tell your new best friend Shameka, who's mother should still be in jail? Or you mean you won't tell KNote, who had everything I should have? You take me for a fool?"

Hazel's heart pounded. She had to keep Jenika talking, hoping against hope that KNote or Shameka would realize something was wrong and come looking for her.

"I need to finish you and get out of here. I have all that money from Shanice stashed away. Besides the mustang, I have every penny I took from that miserable woman. I deserved it all."

Jenika leaned closer, her voice cold. "Time to say goodbye, Hazel."

Panic surged through Hazel's chest. Her mind screamed at her to think of something, anything. She met Jenika's eyes and forced her voice to stay steady. "If you kill me, everyone will know it was you. There'll be DNA. Evidence. They'll know it was you. You won't get away with this."

Jenika motioned for Hazel to stand, the syringe still aimed at her. "Text your friends," she ordered. "Tell them you're back at the hotel. I can be across state lines into Illinois before they discover you're missing."

Hazel shook her head. "I won't," she said firmly.

The room fell into a heavy silence, the air thick with unspoken threats. Hazel's pulse thundered, and she prayed her lie would be enough to save her.

"Get up," Jenika urged.

"No," Hazel shook her head defiantly.

Jenika pointed the syringe at her. "I said, get up, now," she said slowly. "This is a much stronger drug than Shanice got and I'm not afraid to use it," pointing the syringe at her.

Hazel's legs trembled as she rose, her mind racing for a way out. She moved slowly toward the door.

"We're going for a little ride," Jenika said, her voice chillingly calm.

Hazel's pulse thundered in her ears as she reached the doorway. She glanced back at the photos one last time. She had to find a way to survive this.

Hazel pushed the door open, her hands trembling as rain lashed against her face. She stepped onto the landing, her soaked shoes squeaking, with Jenika just a step behind her. The rain hadn't let up; it fell in relentless sheets, turning the night into a swirling mess of shadows and sound.

They made their way down the slick steps, moving cautiously, their breaths visible in the cold, damp air. Hazel's heart raced as they approached the car.

Her fingers fumbled with the driver's side handle, and she managed to pull the door open, glancing over her shoulder at Jenika.

Before she could say a word, flashing red and blue lights flooded the driveway. A spotlight snapped on, piercing through the downpour and blinding them both.

The wail of the siren was deafening, but Hazel could still hear the sound of car doors slamming and heavy boots splashing through puddles.

"Jenika! Lyrix, stop right there! We have you surrounded!" barked a gruff voice.

Hazel froze, blinking against the spotlight's harsh glare. Detective Ridley stepped out of the shadows, his gun drawn, his tone steady but unmistakably commanding.

Jenika's grip tightened around Hazel. Hazel felt Jenika's arm snake around her waist, pulling her back against her chest. The cold sting of a needle pressed against Hazel's neck.

"Stay back!" Jenika shouted, her voice shrill and cracking with panic. "I'll kill her! Don't come any closer!"

"Put your hands where we can see them!" Detective Ridley shouted, his voice cutting through the rain like a whip.

Jenika didn't move, her breathing sharp and erratic.

Hazel shivered, her skin crawling where the syringe touched her. "Please, Jenika," she whispered, her voice trembling. "You don't have to do this."

"Shut up!" Jenika hissed, her words frantic. "This is your fault. All of it."

Detective Ridley didn't flinch, his eyes locked on Jenika. "Listen to me, Jenika. No one has to get hurt tonight. Let her go. We can figure this out."

Behind him, another figure emerged from the rain. KNote stepped into the light, her face calm, her gaze piercing. She moved forward slowly, hands raised.

"Jenika," KNote said, her voice softer, gentler. "It's me. Lyrix, it's me. We're sisters."

Jenika's body tensed, her grip on Hazel tightening further. "You're nothing to me!" She spat, her voice venomous.

KNote stopped a few feet behind Detective Ridley, her eyes never leaving Jenika's. "Please," she said softly, her tone pleading. "You don't have to do this. Just let Hazel go."

At once, Hazel knew this was the wrong thing to say.

Jenika let out a ragged laugh, her hand trembling as she pressed the needle harder against Hazel's neck. Hazel whimpered, her knees threatening to buckle beneath her.

"Don't come any closer!" Jenika screamed, her voice cracking with desperation. "I mean it!"

Time seemed to stretch endlessly. The rain pounded harder, soaking everyone to the bone. The air was thick with tension.

Then, it all happened at once.

Jenika's hand jerked, the needle piercing Hazel's skin.

Hazel gasped as a cold numbness swept through her, her body collapsing in Jenika's grip. As her vision blurred and darkness crept in, she heard the crack of gunfire slicing through the storm.

The world around her dissolved into chaos, voices shouting, the rain hammering, and the weight of everything slipping away.

Chapter 29: Monday Afternoon

Hazel's head throbbed with a relentless, pounding ache. A steady, rhythmic beeping pierced through her haze, grating on her nerves. She wanted it to stop. Her entire body ached as if she'd been crushed under the weight of something heavy, and her mouth was so dry it felt like she'd been chewing up sandpaper.

The sharp, antiseptic smell of the room burned her nostrils with every shallow breath. She tried to open her eyes, but her eyelids felt impossibly heavy, as though they were weighted with lead. Somewhere in the haze of her mind, a voice broke through.

"She's waking up," someone said, the urgency in the tone stirred something inside her.

A light touch grazed Hazel's wrist, followed by something cold and round pressed against her chest. The chill startled her, sending a faint shiver through her otherwise sluggish body.

With monumental effort, Hazel summoned every ounce of strength and forced her eyes open. Blinding white light flooded her vision, and she winced, squeezing her eyes shut again, the ache in her skull intensifying.

"You're okay," said the voice, soft but firm, its tone laced with relief.

Hazel hesitated. The voice was familiar but distant, like a memory struggling to surface. She tried again, squinting against the light until the blurry shape of a face came into focus. Recognition hit her like a jolt.

"KNote?" Hazel rasped, her voice raw and barely audible.

KNote's face broke into a wide smile. Her cheeks were streaked with tears, and her eyes shone with an overwhelming mix of emotions. "We thought we lost you," she choked out. She clasped Hazel's hand tightly.

Another voice joined in, warm and steady. "We're so relieved you're okay." Shameka leaned in, her hand gently wrapping around Hazel's other one.

Hazel blinked, the sight of their worried faces grounding her in reality. "Where...?" She tried to speak, but the words scraped painfully against her raw throat.

"Get her some water," KNote urged.

Shameka moved quickly. She grabbed a cup and guided the straw gently to Hazel's lips.

The first sip was heavenly. Cool and refreshing, the water eased the desert in her mouth and throat. Hazel drank slowly, savoring every drop before whispering a hoarse, "Thank you."

She glanced around the room, trying to piece together her surroundings. The bright, sterile space with its bland walls and faint humming of machines confirmed her worst suspicion. "Where am I?"

"You're in the hospital," KNote said gently.

Hazel frowned, her mind foggy. "What happened?"

Shameka exchanged a quick glance with KNote, her face shadowed with worry.

"You've been here since last night," she explained softly. "Jenika injected you with diamorphine, but you're okay. The medics were already there on the scene, and they got to you in time. You were incredibly lucky."

KNote squeezed Hazel's hand gently. "You were so brave," she added, her voice filled with admiration.

"I...I don't remember," Hazel admitted, her brow furrowing. "What happened to Jenika?"

The question hung in the room, tension hanging heavy in the air.

Hazel caught the flicker of concern that passed between KNote and Shameka.

"She's down the hall," KNote finally said. "Recovering from a gunshot wound. Detective Ridley..." she hesitated, a faint smirk tugging at the corner of her lips. "Well, it turns out he's a much better shot than investigator."

Hazel's chest tightened. "So...is she going to be okay?"

"Yes," KNote assured her. "She'll recover. But once she's discharged, she'll be going to prison for a very long time."

A pause followed, each woman lost in her own thoughts.

KNote's voice softened, her eyes glistening with unshed tears. "She's alive, though. And...I still hope, someday, we can build a relationship. We're sisters, after all. Maybe not by blood, but we're connected."

Hazel studied KNote's face, her heart touched by the sincerity in her words. Despite everything Jenika had done, KNote's unwavering hope for reconciliation shone through.

A faint and tired smile tugged at Hazel's lips. "Maybe," she whispered, her voice laced with a blend of doubt but also a glimmer of cautious hope.

The three of them sat in a comforting quiet, their hands entwined as if an anchor for each other. The steady beeping of the monitors filled the silence, the only sound in the room, marking the end of the storm that had raged through their lives.

KNote and Shameka gently squeezed Hazel's hands, their grip speaking volumes where words failed. Gratitude swelled between them, unspoken but undeniable.

Hazel had nearly lost her life unraveling the truth behind Shanice's murder. She had cleared Verna's name, freeing Shameka from the weight of her mother's false accusations. And she brought KNote a sliver of peace by exposing the real killer.

Hazel's eyes grew heavy, her exhaustion impossible to ignore.

Shameka noticed and leaned in with a gentle smile. "Why don't we leave you to rest?" she murmured softly.

Hazel smiled just before her eyes fluttered shut. A deep and peaceful sleep claimed her, and for the first time in what felt like ages, she was surrounded by calm.

Chapter 30: Wednesday

Later, Hazel sat up in her hospital bed, a plastic tray balanced on her lap as she spooned the last bit of strawberry Jell-o from its cup. She placed the tray aside when Detective Ridley walked in.

"How are you feeling, Ms. Whitmore?" he asked, his tone uncharacteristically gentle.

"Like I've been through a storm." Hazel replied. "Things are still a bit fuzzy, but I'm okay."

Detective Ridley's expression hardened. "That was pretty reckless of you."

Hazel raised an eyebrow. "Well, I did solve Shanice's murder. Now you can retire with the case closed," she said, her lips quirking into a small smile.

The detective's mouth twitched, the closest thing to a smile she'd seen from him. "We recovered your 911 call. Good thinking, tapping on the emergency button on your phone. The operator heard everything Jenika said and patched us in. Your quick thinking might have saved your life."

Hazel nodded, gratitude swelling in her chest. "What happens to Jenika now?"

"She's under arrest," Detective Ridley said, his tone grave. "She's being evaluated. It seems like she had a psychotic break. Most likely, she'll be confined to a high-security mental health facility."

Hazel sighed as a wave of sadness washed over her. "She's been through so much. It's heartbreaking that she's all alone."

Detective Ridley nodded but did not respond to Hazel's words. Instead, he glanced at his watch.

"When you're discharged, come down to the station. We'll finalize everything and then you can return home," he said, and turned to leave.

At the door he paused. "And Ms. Whitmore? Nice work."

With that, he walked away, leaving Hazel alone with her thoughts.

Two days later, Hazel found herself in the backseat of a sleek black sedan. She gazed out the window as the car rolled to a stop at the curb. Her chest tightened with a mix of relief and apprehension.

"We're here." Marcus said, shifting the car into park. He stepped out swiftly, opened Hazel's door, and retrieved her heavy suitcase from the trunk.

Hazel adjusted her scarf, took a steadying breath, and stepped out of the car. "Thank you so much, Marcus," she said, flashing him a bright smile.

"Safe travels home, Ms. Whitmore," Marcus replied with a courteous nod before heading back to the driver's seat.

With a firm grip on her suitcase handle and her bags balanced on her shoulders, Hazel turned and walked into St. Louis International Airport. She was going home.

Navigating the crowded terminal, she made it through security and found her gate. Settling into a chair, she untied her scarf and looped it around the handle of her bag. From inside her purse, she pulled out her knitting; the same vanilla stripe sock she'd been working on just a week ago in this very airport. The rhythmic movements of her needles provided a welcome distraction.

But the memories lingered, vivid and unshakable. Every time she closed her eyes, those lifeless gray eyes stared back at her.

Only a week ago, her life had taken a sharp and chaotic turn. It felt like years had passed, yet it had all happened in the blink of an eye.

Hazel glanced around at the bustling terminal. Travelers hurried to their gates, some arriving, others departing. A small smile tugged at her lips as she wondered which of these strange women around her might invade her personal space to touch her knitting without consent.

Hazel didn't quite feel like herself yet. She'd survived a storm, uncovered the truth, and brought justice for Shanice.

Whatever came next, she was ready. And Whitley would be there waiting.

Chapter 31: Epilogue (6 Months Later)

Hazel woke early, eager to steal a few quiet moments in the parlor before the mansion came to life with the energy of the retreat. Morning sunlight streamed through her window, deceptively warm against the lingering chill of early spring in the Berkshires.

She showered and dressed with care, pulling on a crocheted sweater from her book, *Sweaters That Fit*. She'd made a few tweaks to the original pattern, swapping the fingering weight yarn for a cozy bulky version that hugged her in warmth.

The book had been a labor of love, and this retreat was an honor. Hazel was here to mentor aspiring designers, to be the kind of guide she had once needed. The role felt both surreal and humbling. After a final glance in the full-length mirror, she grabbed her scarf, notebook, and current project, ready for the day.

The grandeur of the mansion had enchanted her when she arrived the day before. She'd spent the evening at a fireside chat with the mentees, marveling at their enthusiasm and ambition.

Today would be packed with small-group workshops, but this quiet morning was hers. She wanted to soak in the serenity of the parlor and make progress on her next book, inspired by the retreat's beautiful setting.

Her footsteps echoed softly as she descended the grand staircase, a light skip in her step. But halfway down, she stopped cold on the landing.

A figure stood at the base of the stairs, cloaked in dark clothes, a hood pulled low over their head. They faced the door, speaking into a phone pressed tightly to their ear.

"I don't know where she is," the voice said, sharp and urgent. "I found her phone, but not her. I'm going to keep looking."

Hazel's stomach twisted. Her early calm evaporated, replaced with a creeping sense of dread.

It had taken everything in her to come to this retreat. For months, she'd hidden away, finding solace in the safety of home, far from the memories of gray, lifeless eyes that haunted her whenever she closed her own.

When this opportunity arose, she hesitated, questioning whether she could face the world again. It wasn't until she learned what the retreat was about—mentorship, creativity, and connection—that she found the courage to say yes.

And now, this. Something had happened.

The figure ended the call and turned slowly. Their gaze met Hazel's, and recognition flashed between them. Her chest tightened.

She knew something was terribly wrong.

Her eyes darted to the main room on the ground floor, where a small cluster of people stood. Their grim faces and tense postures confirmed her worst fears.

Hazel's pulse quickened, her thoughts racing as the figure took a step toward her.

Not again, she thought.

THE END

DON'T MISS OUT!

Click the link below and sign up to receive email updates from Tian Connaughton when she publishes new books and patterns. There's no charge and no obligation.

tianconnaughton.kit.com/tianwrites

ABOUT THE AUTHOR

TIAN CONNAUGHTON is a crochet and knit designer, technical editor, coach, and author. With over a decade of experience working with major brands and world-class designers in the fiber industry, she is on a mission to highlight and amplify the stories of historically underrepresented voices.

Tian lives in rural Western Massachusetts with her husband, son, 4-legged fur babies, and a coop full of hens.

Learn more about Tian and her work at www.tianconnaughton.com.

ACKNOWLEDGMENTS

I am deeply grateful to the talented individuals whose contributions played an integral role in bringing this novel to life. Their dedication and expertise have enriched the pages of this book, and I am truly thankful for their support.

First and foremost, I extend my heartfelt appreciation to Samantha M. Ryan [Copy Editor], whose attention to detail and keen editorial insights have polished this manuscript to perfection.

A special thank you goes to Madelyn Fischer [Book Cover Designer] for crafting a visually stunning and captivating cover that beautifully captures the essence of the story within.

Thank you all for being an essential part of this creative process and contributing to the realization of this novel.

Books by Tian Connaughton

- The Magic Knitting Pattern Book (a novel)

- Cardigans For Every Body: because every body is worthy

- Unlock Your Inner Designer: How to start designing

- Pattern Launch Plan: Sell more patterns consistently without being sleazy

tianconnaughton.com/books

PATTERN: Broken Glass Scarf

PATTERN DESCRIPTION

The Broken Glass Scarf is worked back and forth in one piece, from tip to tip, in a cable and lace stitch pattern with built-in i-cord edges. Choose one skein of your favorite DK weight yarn to knit this small scarf. The size is easy to customize by knitting more repeats of the Even Section or start decreasing earlier for an extra small scarf.

SKILL LEVEL

Adventurous Beginner / Intermediate

FINISHED MEASUREMENT

3" (8 cm) wide x 48" (122 cm) long

MATERIALS

Yarn: Lonnie Bunny's Enchanted Yarns (dk weight)

Knight DK (60% Superwash Merino, 20% Yak, 20% Silk; 4ply/ 231 yards/100 grams)

1 skein Enchanted Encore

Needle: US Size 10 (6mm)

Extras: Cable Needle, Tapestry Needle

GAUGE

17 sts x 1 pattern repeat = 3" (8 cm), blocked

Gauge is not crucial to this project, BUT it will affect the finished measurement of the scarf and how much yarn needed.

ABBREVIATIONS

BO - Bind off

CO - Cast on

C3F (Cable 3 Front) - Slip next 2 sts to cable needle and hold to front of work, knit next st from left needle, knit two sts from cable needle

DEC - Decrease

INC - Increase

K - Knit

K2TOG - Knit two stitches together

M1 (increase) - Make one

P - Purl

SL - Slip

SSK – Slip, slip, knit

ST(S) - Stitch(es)

WYIF - With yarn in front

YO - Yarn over

PATTERN NOTES

The Broken Glass Scarf is a fun little accessory for all seasons. This skinny scarf is the perfect quick knit, using only one skein of your favorite DK weight yarn. The small scarf wraps beautifully around the neck as a dainty ascot or a flirty headband. The instructions are easy to follow with simple stitches.

INSTRUCTION

GARTER SECTION

CO 4 sts.

Rows 1-3: Sl1 wyif, k1, sl1 wyif, k1.

INCREASE SECTION

Note: In this section, increase one stitch every other row until there are 17 stitches on the needles.

Row 1 (Inc): Sl1 wyif, k1, m1, sl1 wyif, k1. (5 sts)

Row 2: Sl1 wyif, k2, sl1wyif, k1.

Row 3 (Inc): Sl1 wyif, k1, p1, m1, sl1 wyif, k1. (6 sts)

Row 4: Sl1 wyif, k1, p1, k1, sl1 wyif, k1.

Row 5 (Inc): Sl1 wyif, k1, p1, k1, m1, sl1 wyif, k1. (7 sts)

Row 6: Sl1 wyif, k1, p2, k1, sl1 wyif, k1.

Row 7 (Inc): Sl1 wyif, k1, p1, k2, m1, sl1 wyif, k1. (8 sts)

Row 8: Sl1 wyif, k1, p3, k1, sl1 wyif, k1.

Row 9 (Inc): Sl1 wyif, k1, p1, k3, m1, sl1 wyif, k1. (9 sts)

Row 10: Sl1 wyif, k2, p3, k1, sl1 wyif, k1.

Row 11 (Inc): Sl1 wyif, k1, p1, C4F, m1, sl1 wyif, k1. (10 sts)

Row 12: Sl1 wyif, k2, p4, k1, sl1 wyif, k1.

Row 13 (Inc): Sl1 wyif, k1, p1, k4, p1, m1, sl1 wyif, k1. (11 sts)

Row 14: Sl1 wyif, k1, p1, k1, p4, k1, sl1 wyif, k1.

Row 15 (Inc): Sl1 wyif, k1, p1, k4, p1, k1, m1, sl1 wyif, k1. (12 sts)

Row 16: Sl1 wyif, k1, p2, k1, p4, k1, sl1 wyif, k1.

Row 17 (Inc): Sl1 wyif, k1, p1, k4, p1, k2, m1, sl1 wyif, k1. (13 sts)

Row 18: Sl1 wyif, k1, p3, k1, p4, k1, sl1 wyif, k1.

Row 19 (Inc): Sl1 wyif, k1, p1, C4F, p1, k3, m1, sl1 wyif, k1. (14 sts)

Row 20: Sl1 wyif, k1, p4, k1, p4, k1, sl1 wyif, k1.

Row 21 (Inc): Sl1 wyif, k1, p1, k4, p1, k4, m1, sl1 wyif, k1. (15 sts)

Row 22: Sl1 wyif, k1, p5, k1, p4, k1, sl1 wyif, k1.

Row 23 (Inc): Sl1 wyif, k1, p1, k4, p1, k1, k2tog, k2, yo, m1, sl1 wyif, k1. (16 sts)

Row 24: Sl1 wyif, k2, p5, k1, p4, k1, sl1 wyif, k1.

Row 25 (Inc): Sl1 wyif, k1, p1, k4, p1, k2tog, k3, yo, p1, m1, sl1 wyif, k1. (17 sts)

Row 26: Sl1 wyif, k3, p5, k1, p4, k1, sl1 wyif, k1.

EVEN SECTION

Note: This section is worked evenly over 17 stitches without increasing or decreasing.

Row 1: Sl1 wyif, k1, p1, C4F, p1, yo, ssk, k3, p2, sl1 wyif, k1.

Row 2: Sl1 wyif, k3, p5, k1, p4, k1, sl1 wyif, k1.

Row 3: Sl1 wyif, k1, p1, k4, p1, yo, k1, ssk, k2, p2, sl1 wyif, k1.

Row 4: Sl1 wyif, k3, p5, k1, p4, k1, sl1 wyif, k1.

Row 5: Sl1 wyif, k1, p1, k4, p1, yo, k2, ssk, k1, p2, sl1 wyif, k1.

Row 6: Sl1 wyif, k3, p5, k1, p4, k1, sl1 wyif, k1.

Row 7: Sl1 wyif, k1, p1, k4, p1, yo, k3, ssk, p2, sl1 wyif, k1.

Row 8: Sl1 wyif, k3, p5, k1, p4, k1, sl1 wyif, k1.

Row 9: Sl1 wyif, k1, p1, C4F, p1, k3, ssk, yo, p2, sl1 wyif, k1.

Row 10: Sl1 wyif, k3, p5, k1, p4, k1, sl1 wyif, k1.

Row 11: Sl1 wyif, k1, p1, k4, p1, k2, k2tog, k1, yo, p2, sl1 wyif, k1.

Row 12: Sl1 wyif, k3, p5, k1, p4, k1, sl1 wyif, k1.

Row 13: Sl1 wyif, k1, p1, k4, p1, k1, k2tog, k2, yo, p2, sl1 wyif, k1.

Row 14: Sl1 wyif, k3, p5, k1, p4, k1, sl1 wyif, k1.

Row 15: Sl1 wyif, k1, p1, k4, p1, k2tog, k3, yo, p2, sl1 wyif, k1.

Row 16: Sl1 wyif, k3, p5, k1, p4, k1, sl1 wyif, k1.

Repeat these 16 rows 10 more times or until desired length.

DECREASE SECTION

Note: In this section, decrease one st every other row until 4 sts remains on your needles.

Row 1 (Dec): Sl1 wyif, k1, p1, C4F, p1, yo, ssk, k3, k2tog, sl1 wyif, k1. (16 sts)

Row 2: Sl1 wyif, k2, p5, k1, p4, k1, sl1 wyif, k1.

Row 3 (Dec): Sl1 wyif, k1, p1, k4, p1, yo, k1, ssk, k1, k2tog, sl1 wyif, k1. (15 sts)

Row 4: Sl1 wyif, k1, p5, k1, p4, k1, sl1 wyif, k1.

Row 5 (Dec): Sl1 wyif, k1, p1, k4, p1, k3, k2tog, sl1 wyif, k1. (14 sts)

Row 6: Sl1 wyif, k1, p4, k1, p4, k1, sl1 wyif, k1.

Row 7 (Dec): Sl1 wyif, k1, p1, k4, p1, k2, k2tog, sl1 wyif, k1. (13 sts)

Row 8: Sl1 wyif, k1, p4, k1, p3, k1, sl1 wyif, k1.

Row 9 (Dec): Sl1 wyif, k1, p1, C4F, p1, k1, k2tog, sl1 wyif, k1. (12 sts)

Row 10: Sl1 wyif, k1, p2, k1, p4, k1, sl1 wyif, k1.

Row 11 (Dec): Sl1 wyif, k1, p1, k4, p1, k2tog, sl1 wyif, k1. (11 sts)

Row 12: Sl1 wyif, k1, p1, k2, p3, k1, sl1 wyif, k1.

Row 13 (Dec): Sl1 wyif, k1, p1, k4, p2tog, sl1 wyif, k1. (10 sts)

Row 14: Sl1 wyif, k2, p4, k1, sl1 wyif, k1.

Row 15 (Dec): Sl1 wyif, k1, p1, k3, k2tog, sl1 wyif, k1. (9 sts)

Row 16: Sl1 wyif, k2, p3, k1, sl1 wyif, k1.

Row 17 (Dec): Sl1 wyif, k1, p1, k2, k2tog, sl1 wyif, k1. (8 sts)

Row 18: Sl1 wyif, k1, p3, k1, sl1 wyif, k1.

Row 19 (Dec): Sl1 wyif, k1, p1, k1, k2tog, sl1 wyif, k1. (7 sts)

Row 20: Sl1 wyif, k1, p2, k1, sl1 wyif, k1.

Row 21 (Dec): Sl1 wyif, k1, p1, k2tog, sl1 wyif, k1. (6 sts)

Row 22: Sl1 wyif, k1, p1, k1, sl1 wyif, k1.

Row 23 (Dec): Sl1 wyif, k1, k2tog, sl1 wyif, k1. (5 sts)

Row 24: Sl1 wyif, k2, sl1 wyif, k1.

Row 25 (Dec): Sl1 wyif, k2tog, sl1 wyif, k1. (4 sts)

GARTER SECTION

Rows 1-3: Sl1 wyif, k1, sl1 wyif, k1.

BO 4 sts.

FINISHING

Weave in all ends.

Block scarf to open up the lace pattern.

Explore Tian's pattern store for more unique designs:
TianConnaughton.com/pattern-store

Did you love *Death by Drop Spindle*? Then you should read *The Magic Knitting Pattern Book*[1] by Tian Connaughton!

[2]

On another visit to her local yarn shop, Asante Jones seeks the comfort and solace of the familiar haven and the perfect yarn for her latest project. In addition to more yarn for her stash, a hidden treasure awaits her in the form of a mysterious antique patterns book, 'The Magic of Knitting Patterns.' Asante begins a new journey as she follows the patterns, seemingly unleashing the book's power.

In her quest for answers, Asante teams up with local historian LaShawn Davie to navigate the threads of history and magic woven into the very fabric of the patterns. As she knits her way through the instructions, she discovers a connection between the designer and a

---

1. https://books2read.com/u/4E7xQg

2. https://books2read.com/u/4E7xQg

stolen painting, adding an unexpected twist to her already captivating journey.

Join Asante and LaShawn in this riveting tale of mystery, magic, and unraveling secrets, where the soothing click of needles becomes a conduit to the unknown, and each knitted stitch reveals a hidden world waiting to be explored. 'The Magic of Knitting Patterns' is not just a book—it's a gateway to a realm where creativity intertwines with the extraordinary.

www.ingramcontent.com/pod-product-compliance
Lightning Source LLC
Chambersburg PA
CBHW072355020726
47506CB00004B/1128